Dr. Tarek Nakhla is an Egypt-born physician, who graduated from the faculty of medicine, Alexandria University, in Alexandria, Egypt. He received medical training in the United States, and is currently practicing in New Jersey. Tarek has authored poems in Arabic and English and co-authored scientific articles. *The Fallen Leaf* is his first novel.

Tarek Nakhla

THE FALLEN LEAF

A non-caregiver's memorable
journey through dementia

AUSTIN MACAULEY PUBLISHERS™
LONDON • CAMBRIDGE • NEW YORK • SHARJAH

Ordering Information
Quantity sales: Special discounts are available on quantity purchases by corporations, associations, and others. For details, contact the publisher at the address below.

Publisher's Cataloging-in-Publication data
Nakhla, Tarek
The Fallen Leaf

ISBN 9781647503642 (Paperback)
ISBN 9781647503635 (Hardback)
ISBN 9781647503659 (ePub e-book)

Library of Congress Control Number: 2023900686

www.austinmacauley.com/us

First Published 2023
Austin Macauley Publishers LLC
40 Wall Street, 33rd Floor, Suite 3302
New York, NY 10005
USA

mail-usa@austinmacauley.com
+1 (646) 5125767

As I embarked on writing, a personal experience that lasted three years but left an everlasting impression on my life, I wondered how the reader would benefit from my experience.

In the beginning, I thought that a one-man's experience with dementia may not seem unique. Still, as I was writing, I realized that this experience affected so many people and has the potential to help many who may encounter similar circumstances. I also realized how thankful I should be to all the people who played a role in this experience. I could not have been able to get through these three years without the support of.

My wife who stood by me and shared with me all the worries and the ups and downs of trying to arrange the care. My two sons who helped with the care of my uncle, inspired illustrations for this book, helped with my uncle's laundry and inspired me every day.

My uncle's sister-in-law who experienced firsthand my uncle's deterioration and saved him from trouble several times before he ended up in the hospital. I could not have been able to arrange the care for my uncle without her generous donation.

My cousins who shared with me the worries of how to arrange the care for my uncle.

The priests and the members of the Coptic Orthodox Church who visited and prayed for my uncle and arranged the funeral.

The professional staff that took care of my uncle; nursing/social workers/aides/nursing home staff/hospice workers/administrators etc.

A simple smile from a person who took care of my uncle made a big difference in how he behaved.

First and foremost, I am thankful to the Lord Who gave me this unique opportunity to witness the vulnerability of us, humans, and how we always need each other to survive.

Table of Contents

Prelude

When an elderly person is stricken with dementia, a need arises for someone to be the caregiver for that person. An immediate family member, or members, would ideally assume that responsibility. Whether it is a wife, a husband, a father, a son, or a daughter, the primary caregiver usually has a good understanding of how the person's life was before dementia. Living with dementia may not seem as bad to the inflicted person as it to the caregiver, who tries to provide them the help, support, and protection they need. The caregiver in that case naturally feels comfortable being the caregiver, taking charge of that person's life, and not questioning how he/she got this authority.

When Amir got the call that his uncle, who had been living by himself, was having troubles, he did not quite understand what was expected of him. His uncle's personal life had been a very private one for many years. Amir immediately learned that his journey with dementia was not going to be the same as others' journeys. He had to become the guardian for his uncle, but he did not have to become the primary caregiver.

It seemed to Amir, who was fifty years old, that he was forced to adopt a child who was seventy-four. There were no adoption procedures, and there were no background checks to ensure that he would be able to take care of his sick uncle. He had to make major decisions for his uncle at a time when he was not interested or ready to do this. Before he was appointed by the court as the guardian, he was expected to make healthcare and financial decisions.

It took some investigation looking for a relative of his uncle, and when they were able to find Amir, they were not going to let him go without becoming the responsible person. Amir writhed trying to fathom what was expected of him, and what he would be expected to do to help his uncle; all that while unsure if his uncle was approving the invasion into his private life. He got used to a role that he called the "non-caregiver" – someone who is not primarily responsible for the day-to-day care but is ultimately responsible for the person's overall well-being. His role also included arranging all the financial needs. He preferred that term over being the "guardian," since he felt that he was not doing enough of "guarding" over every aspect in his uncle's life.

There is no cure for dementia yet, and all that is provided to the patients is support and help until their journey ends. As dementia progresses and becomes associated with other health problems, it is expected that the person's life will be shortened by many complications. Amir's "non-caregiver" role, a journey of almost three years was filled with the thought of, *how long can this go on for?* He initially did not seek an answer to that question, nor did he 'google' it, since he came to realize that his journey with dementia would end when it was meant for it to end, and he just had to wait, and try to do his best.

Although the story of the *Fallen Leaf* was inspired by true events, the names, locations, and the events in the story were not all true, and any resemblance to real names or locations is by mere coincidence.

11

Chapter One
'At the Bus Stop'

It was the beginning of fall, and the school year had already started. With it began the long five or ten minutes of waiting at the school bus stop, where Amir had to wait for his son. The shade from the fully leafed maple tree broke the still, hot weather in September. Amir had been living in the Northeast of the United States for more than twenty-seven years, and still couldn't figure out the season's weather, since every year seemed different. That September of the year 2013, the temperature was still warm compared to the last one. By nature, Amir generally didn't mind the hot weather. When he mentioned this to friends at work, they always associated that to the fact that he was born in Egypt, where the weather was much warmer than in New Jersey. He usually let them to believe that this was true, although he did not entirely believe it. His mother, who passed away a few years before, loved the cold, and she could not stand a hot day in October, let alone July in Cairo. She was born in Cairo and moved to Alexandria when she got married to his father. The sea breeze of the Mediterranean in Alexandria was probably a factor in her acceptance of marrying someone from another city in the late 1950s.

Why was the bus late today? The school had mentioned that in the first few days of school, there would be some delays while the bus drivers and the students got used to the schedule, but it had already been about three weeks. Amir's phone rang and it was Hoda, his wife. She was back at the house, which was down the hill from where he was standing, and he would not be able to see her even if she came out of the house. She was letting him know that the school sent an email saying that the buses would be late again. Since they did not mention how late they were going to be, he had to wait anyway.

Amir remembered one time when he was in elementary school. His school bus was stuck in traffic for some time, and his parents were so frustrated waiting for him, not knowing what was happening. Back then, there were no emails, cell phones, mass-texting, or even reliable landline phone connections. He could see his neighbor from across the street keeping an eye on his moves, watching if there was any hint that the bus was coming so she could come out to pick up her daughter. He decided to sit down on the short retaining wall in front of the house on the corner where the bus stop was. A branch of a tree was hanging over his head. Without noticing, Amir reached up to a green leaf and pulled it off its branch. Still not thinking, he started cutting the leaf into small pieces, and then threw them on the ground. Just then, he remembered a previous conversation that he'd had with his son earlier, close to the end of the school year.

"Dad, why did some leaves fall when it's not fall yet?"

"Don't know, Mikey, I guess it just happens."

He remembered his son bending down and picking up a leaf. "I'll take this one, and it's still green."

"What are you going to do with it?" Amir asked.

"I'll protect it."

"What does this mean?"

"I don't know. I know I can't keep it green for very long, but I'll clean it and watch it dry out in my room."

Amir recalled that in his mind he thought it was going to be a long summer. Although he loved the summers, the thought that he and his wife had to try to entertain the kids made him always welcome the beginning of the next school year. Since his wife had not been working for the last few years, his job had been a little easier during the summers. She was coming up with ideas almost on a daily basis for them to pass the time. This was not an easy job because of the difference in age between Johnathan, his sixteen-year-old son; and Mikey, the six-year-old. The vacation time that Amir took was used for traveling. Their favorite place to go was the beach on the west coast of Florida. Now that the summer was over, he was especially welcoming the beginning of this school year. He needed some time to figure out what he had to do for his uncle Nasseem – his late mother's brother, who lived by himself in Long Island, NY.

Uncle Nasseem Aziz's problems had started earlier that year in May, just after he had landed at JFK Airport in New York. He was coming from his long trip from Cairo, Egypt. For Uncle Nasseem, this was supposed to be the same routine trip that he had gotten used to for the previous eight years. Ever since he retired, every November he would go to Egypt and spend five to six months there.

Amir was not sure exactly why his uncle was spending such a long time away and making these long trips at his age. Nasseem lived by himself in a subsidized one-bedroom apartment on Long Island, NY and managed to be independent. When he went to Egypt, he stayed in his old childhood house, which was a huge apartment in Cairo. As most apartments in Egypt, it did not have heat or air conditioning and was very hard to keep clean. His apartment on Long Island was in a quiet suburban area and it was near supermarkets and a shopping mall, all within a short driving distance.

In Cairo, the apartment that he stayed in, just like most of the cities in Egypt, was on a noisy and busy commercial street. In order for him to be able to get what he needed, he had to take a long cab ride through the very crowded streets of Cairo. There must have been something about going back to where he used to live as a child that made him not mind these long trips. Amir's mother, who was the oldest of her siblings, grew up with her two brothers in that apartment in Cairo before she moved to Alexandria. Nasseem was her youngest brother and her other brother Karim lived in that apartment with Nasseem until Nasseem moved to the United States forty-something years before, leaving Karim in that apartment by himself. Karim eventually died, leaving the apartment empty, except for the times when Nasseem went. The three siblings had three other half siblings who all were deceased; one of them was Dr. Ibrahim Aziz who also lived on Long Island, NY before he passed away. After his sister and his brother died, Nasseem became the only living sibling. Nasseem and his late half-brother, Dr.

Ibrahim Aziz, were the only ones among their siblings who immigrated to the United States.

Every year, Nasseem came back to NY to a car that would not run, having been idle for six months, and needed to re-activate his telephone and cable services. When Amir would ask him about who took care of his mail or who kept track of his bank account, making sure that his social security was deposited on time, he would not give him an answer; so Amir stopped asking. Living in NJ, Long Island, NY was three hours away with good traffic, and with Amir's work and family commitment, he was not able to regularly visit his uncle ever since he moved to southern New Jersey.

That May of 2013, when Nasseem landed in NY, was different from previous years. Debbie, his sister-in-law, the widow of his late brother Dr. Aziz, who also lived on Long Island in NY, got a call from an airport worker saying that he had a man that just landed at JFK who is speaking in a foreign language that they did not understand, and he gave them her number to call. Nasseem lived in the US for more than forty years. Although his English was poor in the beginning, he learned the language and was proficient in it. He had a master's degree in safety engineering from NYU and yet that time, he could not make the switch from Arabic to English.

For someone who only speaks one language, this may not be easy to comprehend but to Amir, hearing that Nasseem was not able to communicate in English was rather understandable. Amir himself found that he occasionally had to catch himself before starting to speak Arabic upon arriving from trips to Egypt. He always wondered how the human brain handles this transition. You go to the airport in Cairo and talk to everyone in Arabic, then you sit for more than ten hours on a flight going through interrupted naps, reading Arabic newspapers, watching Arabic shows on the screens and then you land in a different country, in a different time zone, and you are supposed to be thinking right and instantly start speaking a different language. It is not that easy! This was one of the breaking points for Nasseem; there might have been other problems that happened during this last trip. He arrived in the United States unable to communicate with people, and Amir did not know anything about this until later.

Amir was awakened from his deep thoughts by the sound of the school bus making the turn coming up the hill and turning into his street. He said "Hi" to his neighbor who rushed out of her house carrying her infant daughter to pick up her other daughter. Mikey came off the bus and greeted Amir who started asking him how his day was. He used to be excited to come home to find his older brother who, being in high school arrived earlier. Amir went inside the house and he and his wife started talking about the bus being late and whether it will make sense to just pick him up from school instead of waiting at the bus stop.

Chapter Two

"Debbie Went to Mexico"

How and why did Nasseem only remember that the person that could help him would be Debbie, who was the widow of his late brother, Dr. Ibrahim Aziz? Ibrahim was his older brother that sponsored him to immigrate to the United States forty-something years earlier. Dr. Aziz's address and his phone number were etched in his memory for many years. In fact, Amir also could relate to that. Of all the ever-changing phone numbers and addresses that Amir had in the US, Uncle Ibrahim's number and address he never forgot. At the airport, Nasseem could not find two of the three bags that he checked in, and when they helped him to get a cab the address, he gave was Debbie's address.

He showed up at Debbie's doorsteps with the cab driver who spoke Arabic (nothing that is hard to find in NY). When the driver needed his money, he was about to pay him in Egyptian Pounds. Debbie had to step in and help him pay the driver in US Dollars. He was concerned that he had lost two of his suitcases although he only had one baggage claim ticket in his pocket. Debbie drove him to his apartment, not knowing that this was the start of his problems in the days to come.

Amir knew the day on which Nasseem was supposed to arrive in the US. Amir'ssister who still lived in Egypt told him. As usual, he had to wait for him to call him. Since he always disconnected his phone line before he traveled, almost always he got a new number when he reactivated the service. When Amir finally got a call from Nasseem, he made sure to save his new number. Amir started asking about his trip and sensed unhappiness in Nasseem's voice. He told him that he was not happy because he lost two of his bags and came home with one bag only. Later, Amir found about the confusion at the airport when he spoke to his sister in Egypt who had learned about it from Debbie. One of the missing bags were later found and delivered to Debbie's address, which he gave at the airport. The other bag remained a mystery and most likely did not even exist.

Since Nasseem lived by himself for such a long time, there were many things that Amir did not know about his life. Amir was used to not getting an answer from his uncle if he asked him a question that Nasseem did not want to answer. Nasseem had put limits on what he would share with others, including Amir. Amir always thought that this was odd since the only relatives that Nasseem had in the United States after his brother passed away were his three Nephews and Debbie.

Debbie had two sons.

Tom who also lived on Long Island and Matt who lived in Mexico. The mystery of the lost bag was one of these questions that Amir thought at that time that Nasseem did not want to tell him much about. He did not think too much about that until he called Amir one day asking him to call his nephew in Egypt to search for the bag in the apartment in Cairo. When Amir asked Nasseem who drove him to the airport in Cairo and whether he had the bag as carry-on or checked-in, he never got an answer. At that time, Amir did not suspect that there was a problem; he thought that this was a typical Uncle Nasseem's behavior. Little did he know, that this was only the beginning of what he will have to deal with from now on. Afterwards, it did not take long for Amir to realize that there is something different about Nasseem and he had to start differentiating between what he knew of the old Nasseem and what he had to start dealing with, with the "new" Nasseem.

When Amir's mother was married and moved from Cairo to Alexandria, Nasseem was only seventeen. He was her youngest brother; the "baby" in his family. Nasseem became more dependent on immediate family members after the death of his father. Like Nasseem, Amir was also the youngest of three siblings. Nasseem was twenty-three when Amir was born. As a child, Amir grew up seeing Uncle Nasseem around as a funny and a pleasant adult figure who was so much different from his serious and strict dad. Nasseem was the one who tried to get the attention of any good-looking girl that he saw on the street despite his otherwise well-behaved manners. As a child, Amir saw Uncle Nasseem as a handsome gentleman liked by many girls. Later, he learned that during Nasseem's college years, he had trouble keeping a long-term relationship with any of the girls he met. The years went by without getting married and after his parent's death and immigrating to the US, he lived by himself almost the rest of his life.

Coming to a foreign country, it seemed reasonable that Nasseem needed the help and support of his brother,

Ibrahim, who was a physician that established a career in internal medicine on Long Island, NY. It felt that he always needed the help of someone and Ibrahim and his Italian/American wife, Debbie, were always supporting him. Nasseem gradually realized that he needed to work a little harder to secure a job and he did. He obtained a master's degree in safety engineering from NYU. He worked for an insurance company for seven years before he was laid-off and then things became tougher since he could not find another job in his profession and started to search for any other kind of job that he could do.

Amir arrived in the United States sixteen years after Nasseem, filled with worries and hopes that he will be able to make it in a foreign country. He had just graduated from medical school in Egypt and was hoping to find a residency program that will not only accept him but will also provide him with a special visa that will allow him to stay in the United States. Amir thought that his uncle who had been in America for more than sixteen years will be of big help. He soon realized that the Uncle Nasseem that he knew growing up was suffering after being laid off and was not going to be of much help when he needed him. Amir was a bit disappointed but not surprised and just accepted the fact that he could not ask Nasseem for much. On the other hand, uncle Ibrahim and his wife were instrumental to him in finding a residency position and were supportive to him although he thought they did not know him as well as Uncle Nasseem did.

When Amir called his nephew in Egypt to ask him to check if Nasseem left the bag in the apartment in Cairo, his nephew told him that there was nothing in the apartment.

Amir called him to tell him what his nephew told him. Still, he never told him anything about what happened at the airport and that he went from the airport to Debbie's house because he never remembered his address. Amir believed that one reason he never remembered his address was that ever since he moved to this new apartment, he got a PO Box in the post office in the town next to his town and he always used his PO Box as his mailing address.

Few days later, Amir got a call from Nasseem asking what his phone number and address were because someone asked him and he did not know. Amir started to realize that something was not right with Nasseem and that it was time to visit him to figure out what was happening.

When Amir later got the word about all that happened to him at the airport from Debbie and she mentioned that she thought that he was starting to have early dementia, Amir felt that he needed to visit him sooner than later. Nasseem called Amir several times again asking about his phone number and seemed confused about what day of the week it was. One day he called him to ask him how to get to his barber because he needed a haircut, so Amir searched it on *MapQuest* and tried to give him the directions over the phone, but he did not seem to get it. Another day he told Amir that he had an appointment with his doctor and when Amir called him later to check on him, he said to him that he could not get to the doctor's office. His reason was that he could not find it. Amir confirmed with him several times that he will be visiting on June 20 at about eight o'clock in the morning.

In order to go to Long Island from NJ, Amir had to take the day off from work. On the first day of his older son's summer vacation, he drove with him to see Uncle Nasseem knowing that he might need an extra hand to help him out at his apartment. Having sensed the confusion that he had, Amir expected Nasseem not to be ready at the time of their arrival in NY. To their surprise, he was already awake and dressed. The day before they went, Amir bought some cleaning supplies knowing that his place could be a mess and got some food in case he did not have much at home. They stopped on the way and got some coffee before they went to his apartment. As expected, when Amir and Johnathan entered the apartment, they could not find a place to sit. It was a studio with enough space for them, but each spot was covered with papers and pieces of mail. They washed three dishes, prepared three sandwiches and sat down to have breakfast. Then Amir was trying to figure out what they could do to help him during the next few hours that they were there. Within a few minutes, Amir realized that Nasseem was in desperate need to wash his clothes.

The closets were filled with trash bags that were filled with dirty clothes that Amir felt were there for months. The fridge had food that appeared to have been there since November, before he went to Egypt. He soon realized that they will not be able to do much, and they had to prioritize. They collected all the clothes that needed to be washed and headed to the Laundromat. Although Amir had brought with him detergent, Nasseem did not want to use the one they got him and had to ask to stop by the supermarket to get the detergent of his choice. This was typical of the "picky" Uncle Nasseem that Amir was used to. They spent about three hours at the laundromat then they went to Burger King for lunch. Of course, Amir's idea of bringing

Johnathan with him turned out to work well. His teenage son was able to give him the proper directions using the phone's GPS while he drove. Obviously, he could not rely on Uncle Nasseem for directions.

Everything that day was in slow motion, which was not different from what Uncle Nasseem was used to. They were able to squeeze in some food shopping at Costco and got him some of his favorite items; roasted chicken, *Jarlsberg* cheese and a watermelon. However, because of the time, they could not go anywhere else. When they went home, they cut the watermelon for him and put it in the fridge. They left him that evening not knowing how he had been functioning by himself and how he was going to function from now on. Amir was still thinking that part of it was the Nasseem that he knew for years who asked for help all the time, and part of it was the "new Nasseem."

After Amir's trip to LI with his son in June, he could not go back to check on him. During the school summer vacation, he hardly did anything other than going to work and finding something to do with his sons. Amir and his wife learned that no house projects could be started or planned on being done while schools are off. Therefore, anytime they thought of something they should do or fix, they would think "September." Trying to find time to see Nasseem was not an exception to the "September" planning. When Amir figured out his September work schedule, he looked for a day that he could take off.

That did not mean that the whole summer went by with no incidents. Amir got a frantic call from Nasseem while he was on vacation in Florida, asking him to call the cable company and pay his bill because there was some "confusion." He struggled with him over the phone trying to understand what had happened, but Nasseem could not answer. His answer was, "It's a long story," the expected, typical response. He called the cable company and found out that Nasseem was late on his payments and they were about to terminate his service. This wasn't the only thing that needed to be straightened out, there were other things. Amir received many phone calls from him asking about what day of the week and what month it was, which confirmed Amir's doubts that he does not even turn on the TV to listen to the news. It proved to him that he was sitting in his apartment not doing anything other than watching videos of his old favorite movies. He couldn't go shopping or even drive the way he used to.

Amir later found out from Debbie that once, she received a call from a woman letting her know that she found Nasseem on the Long Island Expressway next to his car. She told her that she stopped to try to help him because he seemed confused and disoriented; luckily, he was able to give her Debbie's number. Debbie ended up asking the police to bring him over to her house. Despite his confusion, Debbie told Amir that Nasseem on that day was able to drive back to his apartment from her house. Once again, she received a call from the owner of a diner in Long Island telling her that Nasseem went there in a cab and he was sitting there, and the owner needed to close and when he asked him to leave, he gave him her number.

Amir didn't find out about these summer instances from Debbie until later when she called to tell him that she would be traveling to Mexico to visit her son, Matt. It turned out that Debbie had been going to Nasseem's apartment once a week to help him. She also helped him schedule for an eye procedure. She was going to be away for three weeks and she thought it would be a good idea if Amir took him to see a neurologist. Amir had decided to go on September 17 and luckily, he was able to get an appointment with a neurologist for that day. His intention was that he will discuss his memory issues with the neurologist so he would recommend home care, so that Amir would feel better that somebody will be checking on him. Since Nasseem complained about a sensation problem in his fingers every time he called Amir, he thought if he told him that he was taking him to see a neurologist, it would make sense to Nasseem. It turned out that trying to explain anything to Uncle Nasseem was becoming an impossible task. There were only certain things that he could understand and remember.

Aside from the fact that Amir was worried about Nasseem during the summer, he was having some health problems that started after he came back from their trip to Florida. He was complaining of nausea and threw up several times without a good reason. Being a physician, Amir always thought of the worst-case scenario. He was a Neonatologist and only worked in the neonatal intensive care unit and his patients were just newborns who were premature or sick. His connection with adult medicine was long lost ever since he started his pediatric residency more than twenty years earlier. This did not prevent him from thinking the worst; a stomach or colon cancer. All the tests that he went through came back negative and he was starting to regain some of his appetite. He was still waiting to have an upper endoscopy on the 24th. He was dealing with all these worries while he was thinking of what he was going to do for Nasseem.

The way the events came about over the next ensuing days was very strange in a sense and nicely planned from heaven. Debbie told Amir to postpone his September 17 visit to Nasseem since she was still going to be around until the 16th. She was going to Mexico to visit her son from September 16 till October 6. Before she left, she called Amir and told him that she took Nasseem out for a haircut and grocery shopping and he should be okay for a while. Amir was able to change the neurologist appointment to the 25th and told Uncle Nasseem. All he had on his mind when Amir spoke to him was, "Debbie is leaving and Amir is coming on the 25th." He told Amir that when he came, he wanted him to help him with the laundry and Amir got the hint that he had probably not done the laundry since his last visit in June. Nasseem didn't know that Amir was having health problems himself and he was going to have the endoscopy done on the 24th to find out if he had any kind of stomach ulcer or growth.

After Debbie left, Nasseem called Amir to confirm that he was coming on the 25th and Amir reminded him that he needed to be ready to leave to go to the doctor as soon as he arrived. Amir was reassured knowing that Debbie had helped him get enough food to last for a while. He believed at that point that all what Nasseem needed was some kind of home care so that someone would check on him and help him. He had discussed it with Nasseem over the phone one time. When Amir opened that subject with him on the phone telling him that he needed to find someone to help him or live in an assisted-living community, Nasseem was not receptive and was very resistant to that idea altogether. Nasseem did not seem to Amir to have a major medical need but he knew he needed help. Something that Amir did not have the ability to provide while he was 140 miles away. Amir even called the neurologist's office ahead of time to see if he could speak to the physician that was going to see him on the 25th to give him a heads up regarding Nasseem's memory issues. His plan was to ask the doctor to recommend home health aide and convince him that it was necessary. Amir did not know that the heaven's plans were different from what he had planned.

One week before the planned visit, Amir was at work in the hospital when he suddenly noticed a voice mail on his cell phone. He had been having trouble with his cell phone dropping some calls. He did not recognize the number and when he opened the voice mail, he was surprised that it was from his cousin, Matt who was in Mexico. Amir wondered that Matt never called him before and how did he even get his number? Then he remembered that Debbie was visiting him in Mexico, so she had his number with her. In the voice mail, Matt said, "Uncle Nasseem is in the Hospital in LI." When Amir called him back, he told him that a social worker at the hospital contacted Tom, his brother, and told him that Nasseem was at Winthrop Medical Center. The story started to unfold little by little, but it never became clear since the main player was Nasseem who, by nature, never clarified anything and now with his new problems, nobody could get any answer from him.

When Lori, the social worker at the medical center asked him who she could contact from his family to tell them that he was in the hospital, he answered: "Debbie went to Mexico," and that was his answer over and over. This time he did not give her Debbie's phone number or address as he used to do whenever people asked him. He 'remembered' that Debbie was in Mexico, so she was not around to answer the phone. He knew that Amir was coming but Amir's phone number was not something that he would remember. It was written on a piece of paper along with the other piles of papers on his desk, yet he had managed to find it many times. This time, he was not in his apartment so calling Amir was not something that was possible.

Chapter Three
'Please Take Me Home'

After two days in the hospital, not knowing who to contact, Lori, the social worker, decided to search (*google*) for someone with the same last name on Long Island. Luckily for Nasseem, Aziz is not a common last name and when she googled it, she was able to find his nephew, Tom Aziz's home number. She spoke to his babysitter, who then called his wife at work, who then emailed Matt to tell him. Matt then called Amir since Tom was out of town and nobody else, but Amir could try to figure out how to help Uncle Nasseem. Although it was still not very clear, the story was that the state police found Nasseem on Sunrise Highway near his car and when he appeared confused, they took him to the hospital, and he was admitted.

Amir got the social worker's number and called her to at least let her know that his family became aware that he was in the hospital. For the next couple of days, Amir was in a loss, he did not know what to do. First, he needed his procedure done on the 24th since he was still having stomach problems. After several conversations with the social worker at the hospital, Amir realized that the hospital needed somebody to come and just take him. They knew he was confused and could not live by himself, and they were so relieved that someone could come and take him. For a little while, Amir thought that the plan could remain the same. He goes to the hospital to pick him up, take him to the neurologist appointment, and then take him home. When Tom was back in town, Amir started talking and texting him about what they should be doing. Tom had a very busy schedule, he could not even get to the hospital, and Amir had already planned on going on the 25th.

Amir was able to call the floor that Nasseem was on and get him on the phone. When Nasseem answered the phone and found that it was Amir, he asked him when he was coming to take him home. It was not a question of "if he was coming?" it was "when was he coming?" In the beginning, Amir told him that he will be coming on the 25th and he will take him home. As Amir was trying to make sense of what made Nasseem admitted to the hospital, he started to realize that his plan was not going to work. Clearly, Nasseem needed more supervision; he could not be by himself at home. Amir spoke to the social worker and told her to tell the medical team that he will visit him, but he was not going to take him.

Where can Nasseem go if he should not go back to his apartment? This was the starting point of how this situation could be handled. Being a neonatologist, Amir knew nothing about taking care of elderly people with dementia, he only knew how to handle and talk to people in the medical profession. He started out by putting the grounds for his decision that Nasseem should not leave the hospital to go home. He needed to be somewhere where he is supervised 24/7. Amir got the feeling that there was some resistance from the staff since the easy way out for the hospital would be releasing him to a family member. Amir could not take care of him. Tom could not do it either and Debbie who was helping him the last few months, did not have the strength to do it anymore. He needed to go to another facility. This was what Amir felt was needed but where and how?

First, Amir needed to visit and tell him that he was only visiting. When he talked to him on the phone, he tried to tell him that he will only come to visit but Nasseem was focused on asking when he was coming to take him. As he was planning his visit to the hospital on Long Island, Amir knew it was going to be a predicament. He had no choice but to go and try to sort things out as much as he could.

It then occurred to Amir that he could use some help from someone else. The only help he could think of at that time was to call the priest of the Coptic Church on Long Island. Amir himself had lived on Long Island a few years before he moved to New Jersey and he used to attend services at that church. This was also something that Amir was used to as he was growing up in Egypt. When there is a problem, you try to get some help from the church. The idea is that even if the problem is not completely solved, you will have someone that will pray for your problem. Prayers are something many times Amir feels bad that he forgets amid trying to fix all the problems by himself. He was able to contact the priest and asked him if he would be able to accompany him during his visit to support Amir as he told Nasseem that he was not there to take him. As he expected, Father Thomas was fast in welcoming the opportunity to visit a sick person in the hospital.

Before he headed to NY, Lori gave him telephone numbers and names of people that can give advice regarding care for the elderly. Amir called one of those numbers which turned out to be a lady that worked for an attorney that she said would help him. The best advice Amir got from her was that the hospital should not force him to take his uncle home. This was Amir's plan at that time; that he needed time to get more information on what his options were. Amir thought that this attorney would be giving him advice. Unfortunately, the attorney was only interested in securing a case, not considering what was best for Amir and Nasseem. Amir knew that he could not make frequent trips to Long Island with his work schedule as it was, and he needed someone to be thinking in the same way. The attorney wanted the case to stay in NY where he practiced.

In everyone's life, there are some days that are hard to forget. Sometimes there are other days that are more important and yet their memories don't remain as vivid. The day that Amir planned to go to the hospital was one that he could never forget. He still could not believe how many things he was able to fit in the eighteen hours from the time he left his house at five o'clock in the morning until he returned just before midnight. The priest had asked him to call him when he got to New York and then he would meet him at the hospital. After Amir had coffee at the Dunkin Donuts across the street from the hospital, he headed to the hospital and waited in the lobby until the priest came. When Father Thomas came, Amir greeted him the same way he always greeted the priests. In the Coptic tradition, you bow down and kiss the priest's hand. The idea behind that is that you show respect and acknowledge that this hand is special as it touches the body of Christ during the liturgy. Amir told Father Thomas the whole story and he asked him to support him if Uncle Nasseem asked to take him home. Amir told him he needed to find out what would work for Nasseem since he cannot be by himself.

Father Thomas looked at Amir in the eyes and again asked him the question that the social worker had asked him over the phone, "You cannot take him with you?"

Like all other times, when Amir responded to this question with a "No," he felt that he was the worst person on this Earth. It was comparable to having the opportunity to serve someone and receive heavenly rewards and you deny that. Based on the Bible teaching, in the Christian faith, if you serve someone in need you are considered serving the Lord. That's why people try hard to find an opportunity to serve someone who is sick or poor. Amir knew that as cruel as the "no" answer to this question sounded, he truly believed that there was no way that Nasseem can go home with him to his house. There was no way that Amir and his family will be able to care for Nasseem and he had it set in his mind that his answer to this question was never going to change under any circumstances. They took the elevator together to the 4th floor where Nasseem was.

As soon as they got out of the elevator, they saw him dressed in a hospital gown standing at the nurses' station. Amir approached him slowly trying to find out what he was asking from the nurse. It turned out that he was complaining that he did not like the breakfast they gave him. The 'royal blood' in him was offended by the type of food he was offered. This was Uncle Nasseem, the man that Debbie, often said that "was certainly born to the wrong family." Uncle Nasseem always acted and tried to appear like royalty. He always would buy expensive brands, brag about a new camera or a shoe or an expensive imported chocolate box that he brought to a gathering and yet everyone knew that he wasn't doing well financially. In fact, as clean as he would look, he was never keen on cleaning the place that he lived in. Amir got the feeling that the Uncle Nasseem that was complaining about his breakfast was not going to take the news about not going home very well.

Amir said "Hi" to him and introduced him to Father Thomas; then they went to his hospital room. It was not a private room and Amir felt from the start that this was a problem for Nasseem who did not like to share places with others. Nasseem did not say much in front of the priest who Amir introduced as coming to check on him since he heard that he was in the hospital. Father Thomas recited a short prayer in the common Coptic tradition and then left them. When Amir and Nasseem were by themselves, Amir tried to get the story of how he ended up in the hospital with no success.

The medical team came to round and he told them he wanted to leave. When they asked him about his address, he said without hesitation, "165 Shobra Street, Cairo, Egypt." Unfortunately, although they realized that he was confused, all what they were concerned about was that he was physically fine so he did not need to be in the hospital and as long as there was someone who could take him, no matter who this person was, they were willing to discharge him. It became apparent to Amir how different adult medicine was from what he practiced. At his work in many instances, the parents of a baby are not allowed to take that baby home if there were questions concerning the home environment or the parent's ability to take care of the child. Nobody even questioned whether Amir was truly his relative. At that moment, Amir realized that he did not actually know why he was even there. It's true that he was his closest relative, but he was not able to take him with him. How could he say that he was responsible of him? He had to go to work and take care of his family, who lived miles away in a different state.

Amir needed to pause and think of what he needed to accomplish in the next few hours. Uncle Nasseem was at least somewhere with some people around and whether they liked it or not, they needed to protect him and take care of him. The list of what he needed to do suddenly grew long in Amir's mind. It felt to him like when he was getting ready to take his wife home from the hospital after the birth of his first son who was born earlier than they expected. Taking a baby home is a nice event that is viewed as a happy occasion despite all the responsibilities it needs. Thinking of assuming a responsibility of an adult who is no longer able to take care of himself is not only physically challenging but also emotionally upsetting.

It did not take long for Amir to figure out what he needed to do.

The social worker asked for Nasseem's documents so she could start working on placement for him and that meant that Amir needed to go to Nasseem's apartment. The nurse showed Amir where they hid the street clothes from him so he would not threaten to leave, and in his pants, Amir found Nasseem's keys and his wallet. Amir then told his uncle that he was going to get him some clothes and some papers from his apartment. He then thought that while he was there, he needed to figure out how he was going to pay his rent, otherwise he could be facing the threat of being kicked out of the apartment. The social worker also asked Amir for a proof of residence and his rent so she can apply for Medicaid for him. She told Amir that one thing they could do was to send him to a nursing home that was affiliated with the hospital so he needed to visit that place to see what it looked like and if they can take him.

Amir took Nasseem's street clothes and left the hospital and told him that he will be back with some clothes for him since he cannot leave the hospital in a hospital gown. Amir now had his wallet, so he had most of the documents that they needed for Medicaid and other things. He was still confused since he did not know if he was legally allowed to make decisions that will affect his uncle's life. He called the attorney to whom he was referred to by the social worker in the hospital and left a message. When he visited the nursing home that the social worker suggested, he felt that it looked like a prison and he needed to find some other place.

The next thing was to get to the apartment and see what was in there that might be useful to bring to the hospital and what documents he could find. On his way to the apartment, Amir started to feel that the way Uncle Nasseem looked and acted without a doubt meant that there was no way that he will be able to live by himself. Amir needed to get from the apartment, each and every thing that would be helpful and to make sure that the rent was paid until he knew what to do next.

While on his way, he got a call from the attorney who was returning his call. Amir asked him how he would be trying to arrange things for Nasseem without any authority and whether he needed to have power of attorney. The attorney told him to ask at the hospital if Nasseem was mentally competent to sign any papers and if they said no then the way to go was to become his guardian. Amir told him that he would get back to him. He called the hospital and asked the social worker to ask the medical team. The social worker got back to him while he was parking the car at the apartment building, telling him that the medical team responded that Nasseem was not competent enough to sign any papers for power of attorney.

As soon as Amir entered the apartment, every corner in that small studio apartment was screaming with signs that this could not have gone on for much longer. The piles of papers on the desk that Amir saw when he visited him with his son three months earlier were still there. Many clothes items were on the floor, including dirty underwear. In the fridge, there were some mold-covered pieces of the watermelon that they got him in June. Amir remembered that Debbie was telling him that before she left to Mexico, she was visiting him every week to take him to the post office to get his mail. She had told him that she had to stop Nasseem one time when he was writing a check. He had in front of him a coupon for oil change and he mistook it for a bill and proceeded to write a check for the amount of money on the coupon. *How in the world Nasseem even managed by himself in the last few months?* He wondered. He recalled that Nasseem called him one time to tell him that he realized that he does not have food in the fridge and Amir told him to go get some before it got dark outside. Did he manage to go and buy something? How did he drive and how did he get back home? Amir started to believe that what happened to his uncle that led him in the hospital was probably the safest thing that could have happened.

Amir spent about an hour in the apartment trying to prioritize what was needed next; pay the rent for the subsidized apartment before it became a problem, make a copy of the key to the apartment in case Nasseem asked for it, and go to the apartment manager to get proof of residence for the Medicaid application. Then Amir found the briefcase. It was the one Debbie had told him about where Nasseem kept all his important documents in. It was an old-fashion *Samsonite* briefcase with a three digits' code lock. Amir had heard from Debbie that he had $3,000.00 in that case. In a hurry, Amir took the briefcase, and some clothes put them in the car and went to have the keys made. He also went to get Nasseem something to eat different from hospital food. He was able to find the address of the apartment management office and went and got the proof of residence from there. He was disappointed after visiting the nursing home suggested by the social worker and found it to be unacceptable. Later in the day, he received a call from Father Thomas who was checking on how things went and advised Amir to not put Nasseem in that nursing home. This confirmed to Amir his feelings about it.

While Amir was going from one place to another, someone at the hospital helped Nasseem make a call to Amir on his cell phone. He was unhappy and annoyed that it was taking Amir such a long time to get back to him; he wanted him to take him home. When Amir got done as much as he could, he headed back to the hospital not knowing how he will be able to handle his uncle. He found him in his room. He started out by telling him that he got him a chicken sandwich hoping that this will distract him from asking about going home. Nasseem told him that he didn't have to because he was leaving soon. Amir asked him for the briefcase combination. As expected, Nasseem was reluctant to do so and started to try to open it by himself but he was not able to concentrate. Again, Amir asked him for the code in *Arabic* trying to hint that no one will understand him. To his surprise he gave him the code, and it was the correct one.

In the brief case, there was Nasseem's passport which was needed for proof of citizenship for the Medicaid application. Amir left the room to go give the papers to the social worker to make copies. When he went back in the room, he was shocked to see that Nasseem had almost finished the sandwich, which was a large one. He felt that his uncle, despite not being able to think very well, was driven by a natural survival instinct. Nasseem then told Amir that they should just leave, and Amir told him that he was not allowed to just take him; he had to wait for the doctor's approval. Nasseem responded that Amir just had to help him take a cab. When Amir asked where he wanted the cab to take him to, Nasseem responded to "165 Shobra street, Cairo, Egypt." At that moment, he had no doubts in his mind that Nasseem needed to be in a nursing home and he couldn't go anywhere else. Amir was able to distract Nasseem and left taking the briefcase with him. He stopped by the social worker to tell her that he will be in touch with her. The social worker that was working on that day was only filling in for Lori, the regular social worker that normally covered Nasseem's floor. Therefore, she told Amir that Lori will be contacting him to follow up.

Having lied to Nasseem several times that day, Amir left the hospital feeling that he had set a new record for the number of lies he told in one day. Before he started on his way back to New Jersey, Amir texted his cousin Tom to get his address, so he could stop by his house first on his way. He wanted to share with someone all what had happened so far. He would have talked to Debbie, Tom's mother, but she was away, and he felt that it was time for him and his cousin to step up to the plate and take care of what was needed to be done. Since Tom lived in NY, he was closer to Nasseem and his apartment, it made sense for Amir to give him the briefcase and Nasseem's apartment key. The next step was to find Nasseem a nursing home. Amir also told Tom that the attorney spoke with him about the need for someone to be appointed the guardian for Nasseem. The attorney said he can take care of this and was going to email him the documents including his fees. It had become apparent to Amir that it was not going to be an easy task going back and forth to NY and he knew that even though Tom lived closer and in the same state as Nasseem, he also was not going to have the time to take care of things.

Back in New Jersey, Amir needed to get back to his normal routine. Going back to work, helping his wife at home and his sons with their homework, but he was so distracted with what he had to do next for Nasseem. The NY lawyer that he spoke with on the phone was still pushing him to get the papers done for him to file for guardianship. Amir still believed that since he wasn't living in NY, this was not possible. It turned out that this was true, and the attorney told him that it had to be Tom who lived in NY. The lawyer made it sound like Tom didn't have to do much. Amir knew that Tom was so busy with his NY job that it wasn't fair to dump this on him, especially that Amir didn't know how much of work and time commitment needed to be put into this. After long conversations with Lori, the social worker at the hospital, Amir realized that it would be much better for Nasseem if he came to a nursing home closer to him in NJ. As simple as it sounded, this was going to create a problem concerning the health insurance and expenses.

In order for Nasseem to be admitted to a nursing home in NJ, he needed to either pay out of pocket or to have Medicaid. Medicaid is state specific so even if they were going to apply for Medicaid for him in NY, this was not going to help if Amir wanted him to be admitted in a New Jersey facility. The solution for this was to find a facility in NJ that will accept him with a Medicaid "pending" application. But what if his NJ Medicaid application was not approved? The cost for his nursing home stay would go to Nasseem or in that case Amir. Amir spoke to several facilities in NJ and none of them were willing to accept him with Medicaid pending.

Lori was after Amir with calls and emails telling him that the physicians are pressuring her to arrange for him to be transferred to a facility in NY which was the easiest thing for them to do. The lawyer called Amir and yelled at him over the phone telling him that transferring Nasseem to a facility in NJ would not work. He said that it will be like Amir was kidnaping Nasseem and making him live in a different state against his will. Amir tried to reason with the lawyer explaining that if Nasseem was closer to him, he would be able to work on the guardianship papers better and he would be able to check on him more often. The lawyer insisted that this would not work, and Amir will end up having to pay a ton of money when the NJ Medicaid gets denied. Lori, on the other hand was understanding and was trying to help Amir but she was also caught in the middle with the treatment team pressuring her to send him to a nursing home since he did not have a "medical" reason to stay in the hospital.

In fact, the medical team was right. Nasseem always took care of his health. He always wanted to get any health problem taken care of, so he never neglected the slightest symptom that he complained of at any time. A small cold would be a big problem that he would consult a physician for and would go to another physician to get a second opinion. Debbie always teased Nasseem about his concern of his health. She always mentioned to Amir that she thought that Nasseem would outlive everyone. "He has at least two doctors for each body organ," she often said.

Amir was at work when he got a call from Lori telling him that she found a facility near Amir's house in NJ and told him that they would take him with Medicaid pending. Amir had already started to lose hope that this will happen. He called that facility right away and spoke to Gina at the Sunshine Rehab center in Sewell, NJ. Gina sounded very nice and told Amir that they will accept him Medicaid pending. She gave him a name of an attorney in NJ to help him with the guardianship. It turned out that Gina was familiar with the process. She told Amir that, for Nasseem to be brought from NY, they needed to get an out-of-state pass and she gave him the contact number for that. Lori told Amir that she could help arrange the transport, but he had to pay for the expenses in advance. Everything was moving smoothly and by that time, Debbie had returned from Mexico and talked to Amir on the phone. Amir told Debbie and Tom not to visit Nasseem in the hospital because he would think that they were going to take him. Especially that he had called Amir several times since he left him and yelled at him that he didn't go back to pick him up and that he also took his street clothes and he couldn't leave the hospital in his hospital gown. Debbie was relieved to hear that Nasseem will be moving to NJ closer to Amir because she was getting worried that she could not take care of his needs anymore.

Although it seemed that there was going to be light at the end of the tunnel, Amir knew that things could not go on without hurdles. Just about when Amir and Lori were almost getting ready to arrange for the transport, Gina called Amir and said to him that the administrators at her center will accept him only if Amir prepaid the first three months until the Medicaid application is processed. This was a huge slap on the face. Three-month worth of care in that facility was $36,000.00 and after what Amir had gone through getting the out of state pass and feeling that things would work well it seemed like they were back to square one. He was at work when Gina told him this and he got so upset.

It was almost four o'clock in the afternoon on Friday and Amir felt that now the NY attorney won. He had warned him that bringing Nasseem to NJ was never going to work. Amir called Debbie to tell her what happened and to tell her that there was no choice now and he will have to put Nasseem in whatever facility they will put him in NY.

To Amir's shock, Debbie said, "No, I don't want him to go to that nursing home near the hospital in NY. I know that it's an awful place." She said, "I'll pay the money."

Amir told her that it was a lot of money, but she said that she would pay it. Now the next thing Amir wanted to do was to update his wife. Hoda was following each step of what he was doing, and he needed to tell her what happened. He knew what her first reaction was going to be. On the phone she just said, "This is too risky, if Nasseem's Medicaid ends up being denied what are we going to do?" Amir did not have an answer for that. He knew that Debbie's gesture, although a very generous one, it carried the fact that she wanted to feel that the burden of taking care of Nasseem was going to be taken away from her and her son and for that, she was willing to pay as much as she could afford.

Amir felt that he had already worked hard on making this happen and he was going to accept any consequences for it, so he accepted Debbie's offer. He called Gina at the Sunshine rehab center back and negotiated that they would only get two months' worth of stay in advance and she asked her administrators and got back to him that they agreed on that. Amir gave Debbie Gina's phone number and she arranged with her how they were going to receive the payment which was in total of $24,000.

Chapter Four
"Nephew, You Are in Trouble!"

Now that Amir was able to have Nasseem accepted into the nursing facility in NJ, he had to arrange for the transport. Amir was stressed out by the fact that Uncle Nasseem will be coming to stay close to his house. His first stress was that he didn't know to what extent Nasseem's brain was functioning. Any man who is in the right state of his mind, who is told to stay in a hospital for a reason he didn't know anything about, then told to be transferred to another "hospital" for the same reason, would easily lose his mind. The expectation then was that a normal person would be upset and would try to get answers. This was how Amir expected Uncle Nasseem to react to his transfer to NJ; lose more of his mind. Amir never doubted that there was something wrong with Nasseem but he always doubted whether things could be done in a different way.

Although Amir was off on the day Nasseem was being transported, he did not want to be at the Sunshine Rehab Center when he arrived. He only wanted to stop by after he was settled in a room so that he would accept that Amir was there to visit and not to take him. After they called him from the center to tell him that his uncle arrived and gave him his room number, Amir had dinner with his family. He packed a dessert to take with him and headed to the nursing center. He stopped at the front desk and asked for his room and was given directions to which hallway he should take. As small as the building looked from the outside, from the inside, the hallways seemed so long and were filled with people who seemed to all have many problems. Patients were lined up in the hallway in wheelchairs and regular chairs just staring at everyone who walked by them. He stopped at the nurses' station where his room was supposed to be.

"I'm here to visit Mr. Aziz. He was admitted this afternoon."

"Are you his nephew?"

"Yes."

"I am Mary Ann, the night supervisor, you are in big trouble!"

"I know, is he not happy?"

"He said you are a doctor and you have a nice big house, he's waiting for you to take him."

Did Uncle Nasseem really remember my house from the time that he visited us six years ago or did he just make this up? Amir wondered as he was walking down the hallway looking for the room. It was not the first time that Nasseem expected Amir to take him. He did that when he visited him at the hospital and Amir was able to get away with it. Was this time going to be different? Did he not do the right thing by putting him in this place?

It was not a pleasant sight, what Amir saw in all the hallways. There were old people everywhere. They looked sad, lonely, and miserable. Some were angry and shouting, some just not talking and some talking to themselves. Others were just by themselves in the rooms. He went into

Nasseem's room and found him lying down on the bed quietly. He did not look happy but was not angry. Amir started by saying that it was a nice room, but he knew that no matter what he would have told him, there was going to be many reasons for him not to like it. The first and most important thing was that there was a roommate, and Uncle Nasseem did not like to be in close contact with people, let alone the ones that he didn't know. He tried to distract him from the fact that he had a roommate by asking different questions.

The strategy that Amir used with his son, who was six at that time, was to distract him from whatever subject he would be talking about to save himself the hassle of explaining or reasoning. This strategy sometimes worked with Uncle Nasseem. Amir tried to help him with figuring out how he will order his food from the menu they gave him and found out times for taking showers. He was able to leave him at that time without any problems. Amir left with some ideas in his mind on what to bring Nasseem next time when he visited that might help him become more comfortable in his new place.

All what was on Amir's mind at that time was how they were going to pay for this nursing facility if his Medicaid application was not approved. He then thought that if the Medicaid approval is the main thing on his mind, why couldn't he share this with Nasseem and put it also in his mind, or whatever was left of his mind. He decided that anytime Uncle Nasseem complained, he would tell him that they must wait until the Medicaid was approved. When he didn't like the room, the answer was, "We have to wait for the Medicaid." He also told him to consider himself in a not so nice of a hotel. Amir continued to try to distract him with something on every visit. He got him a small fridge in his room so that he could bring some food and drinks for him to use when he felt hungry in between meals. When Nasseem complained about the food, the answer was that he had to wait for the Medicaid, and so on.

One of the things that the 'old' Uncle Nasseem was good at was finding ways to get better service when he wanted it. If he went on a trip and didn't like his hotel room, just because, he always found a way to change the room or get something else in return to his dissatisfaction. He could get a free meal or a complimentary upgrade. He was used to being able to get himself heard and get what he wanted. Still, while they were waiting for Medicaid to be approved, Uncle Nasseem found a way to complain and complain and ended up getting a private room. Then when the private room had a bathroom that was shared with the adjacent room, he found a way to complain and got the private room that had its own bathroom. He did all that while Amir was still worried about his Medicaid.

Now that Nasseem was in New Jersey, Amir could apply for NJ's Medicaid. He was extremely worried that it could be rejected, and he would have to face a huge bill from the nursing facility. The person that did the finances in the nursing home had told him that it was just an application and a process. He needed to provide documentations. She promised him that if it got rejected, she could help him find a 'Medicaid' lawyer that could assist him with the process. To start with, she told him that she needed Nasseem's bank statements for the last three years. When Amir was at Nasseem's apartment, he found the statement from *Queens Savings Bank* with his account number on it. Now the challenge was to ask the bank to give Amir three years' worth of statements.

Amir found that it was strange that he had no authority over anything that Nasseem had his name on and yet he was allowed to apply for Medicaid on his behalf. How could he do this when he was not allowed to access Nasseem's account information? He needed to be creative. When he called the bank, they were in some way understanding to the situation but could not help him. After negotiating with the bank manager, they agreed to send him the statements but only to Nasseem's address in NY as long as they also charged his account the fees for sending the statements. The creative part came next; Amir remembered that when his sister-in-law was visiting them from Virginia for extended time, she was able to forward her mail to their address, simply by submitting the request online. That worked, so now Amir saved another trip to Long Island. Not only he got the statements forwarded to NJ but also, he received other mail which included bills and others that he needed to take care of for Nasseem. He later found out that he could have been even more creative by signing him up for online banking.

Gina, at the Sunshine Center, gave him the phone number for the Medicaid office and instructed him to call and make an appointment. He made the appointment. He had learned from Gina that the one thing that Medicaid will look for is a balance that does not exceed $2,000 at any time. They also needed to not see any big deposits and big withdrawals. The one thing that Amir was certain about was that Nasseem's main income came from his social security.

He was able to find out that it was about $1,300, which was good since it was less than $2,000. He then found out that he received a monthly pension from one of his previous jobs in the amount of $120. That was still good because they didn't add up to more than $ 2,000.

Amir remembered something that Nasseem had mentioned to him several years before when he was asking him about how he managed withdrawing his social security money from his account when he traveled to Egypt and stayed there for few months. He acknowledged at that time that this was a tricky situation. For him to stay qualified for the subsidized apartment that he lived in, he also needed to make sure that while he was away his account did not go over the allowed amount of $2,000. He never explained to Amir what he used to do. While he was away, somebody was able to help him out with that, there was no way that Amir was going to be able to find who that person was. Amir's main problem was to be able to show the Medicaid office what they wanted to see in his account; that would make him eligible for Medicaid and then they would pay for his care.

Finding himself in need to be examining his bank statements, trying to speculate or figure out how he managed his spending, seemed very awkward to Amir, but he just had to do it. Gina told Amir, when he got the bank statements to show it to her. It took few weeks and as soon as he got the statements in the mail, Amir went and made a copy and dropped it off at her office. Amir knew that when Nasseem came from Egypt in May of that year and started to have problems, Debbie was helping him with many things, including going to the bank. So, when Amir found out something in the bank statements that happened in July and August and he could not make sense of it, he called Debbie.

The statements showed that he had some money accumulated while he was away. Somehow, when he came back, he went and withdrew $5,000. He then went two days later and deposited that same amount. Then he went back and withdrew it again. This did not make sense.

Amir was aware that few years earlier, Debbie had helped Nasseem get a car instead of the one that used to break down on him and he was supposed to pay her back. She told Amir that she had to go with him to the bank to withdraw the money to take it as partial repayment to her and to help him maintain the $2,000 in his account. Though the story was confusing to Amir, he just had to repeat it in his mind several times so he can believe it and it became his story to explain to anyone. When Gina called him after she reviewed the bank statements to tell him what she found, he was ready with the explanation that Debbie mentioned to him and Gina told him that if Medicaid believed him that would be fine.

When Amir went for the Medicaid appointment, the case worker gave him a list of additional documents he had to get her and submit it within 30 days and then the application would be looked at and a decision was to be made within 60–90 days. It was already at the end of October. Debbie had paid two-month worth of his stay in the nursing center and it was obvious that he will be staying in the center beyond the amount that she paid. Every time Amir thought that he will be waiting all this time just to find out later that the Medicaid was rejected, he would feel sick and depressed. He obviously had no control over this, and he just had to wait. Day by day, he started to realize that plan B, that once crossed his mind, was becoming less realistic. He once had thought that he could use Uncle Nasseem's social security payments to get him an apartment close to where he lived and just check on him from time to time. It was becoming clear to Amir that Nasseem couldn't function at all with no supervision and living by himself somewhere would just not work.

The next few days Amir was gathering everything that the Medicaid needed; including initiating the Guardianship papers. He was facing the challenge of maintaining the $2,000 maximum in Nasseem's bank account. The case worker at the Medicaid office told him that there was no exception to this rule. He did not have any authority over anything that Nasseem had and yet suddenly, he had to be responsible to manage Nasseem's finances. A situation that was too awkward to Amir.

Amir lived his whole life following rules. Honesty was something that occasionally 'put him in trouble' as a child. He was often teased by his sister when he would take his test paper to the teacher to tell her that she made an error in the calculation and his grade should be lower. His sister, and sometimes his parents, thought of this as unnecessary honesty. Amir himself never knew whether this was part of him trying to live by the Christian rules that he had learned as a child or it's just his personality. He had recently gone to a conference where one of his residents was presenting a poster. While he was walking with the resident in the hall in which the poster were to be placed, he ran into one of the attending physicians that was supervising him twenty years before. Dr. Lee greeted Amir with a hug, and he was surprised that she still remembered him. Amir introduced her to the resident that was with him and she turned to that resident and said. "You know Amir was a very good resident. The thing that I remember of him the most is that one time he complained to the chief resident that he was assigned less on-call days during a month and he wanted to be on-call more." Throughout the years, Amir learned to slightly let go of certain things but not without losing some sleep at night when practicality got in the way of honesty.

He now had to convince himself that getting the Medicaid approved was the most important goal and he had to work hard for it. Nasseem's social security money was directly deposited in his account and Amir had to make sure to somehow withdraw it from the account. When he was in Nasseem's apartment, he found only one check book and he had put it in the brief case. He had left it with Tom on the day that he visited Uncle Nasseem in the hospital. It had most of his information. He now needed this brief case. It happened that his sister-in-law was going on a trip to New York, so he arranged for her to meet with Tom and get the brief case. At this point, there were some expenses that he had paid on the way and he felt that if he could just somehow convince Nasseem to sign some checks for him, he would be able to maintain the bank account at less than $2,000 and he could use the money to cover those expenses.

The other thing that he needed to work diligently on was also getting the guardianship papers done. He contacted the attorney that Gina at the center recommended. After several phone calls and emails back and forth, he signed the agreement with the attorney. He had wondered what would happen if he was denied the guardianship and the attorney told him that in that case, the court will have a court-appointed guardian for his uncle. This in a way assured him that this part should not be a problem because why would the court search for someone else when he was willing to be the guardian. He had to pay the attorney the fees to start the process which were about $1,600. These fees were another reason he could use Nasseem's social security money and prevent the account from going over the limit. When he was talking to the Medicaid case worker whom he met on his first visit to the Medicaid's office, he told her that he was working with an attorney for the guardianship papers. She told him that he didn't need an attorney for that, and he could have done it by himself. It was too late, and for him to have worked on it by himself, it would have needed more time when he hardly had enough between trying to figure out this new responsibility along with his work and family obligations.

One of the things that the guardianship papers needed was a statement from Amir describing why he thought he should be the guardian for Nasseem. One more thing that he needed to find the time to sit down and write, yet this was not challenging since sitting down and writing his thoughts was one of the things Amir never minded doing. It didn't take him long to write and writing helped him to gather all his thoughts and come to an understanding on what was happening in his life at that time. He was sure that the attorney did not have to make major changes in what he wrote:

"My name is: Amir Ishak, I am requesting guardianship for my uncle, Mr. Nasseem Aziz because of his worsening dementia.

Mr. Nasseem Aziz, was born on 11/04/1939 in Cairo, Egypt. He had five siblings (one half-brother, two half-sisters, one biological brother and one biological sister). All his siblings are deceased. My mother was his biological sister.

Mr. Aziz immigrated to the United States in the mid-1970s seeking a better opportunity. He obtained a Master's Degree in Safety Engineering and worked in several jobs until he retired. Prior to his retirement he was unfortunate to have some extended periods without employment. He never married and has no children.

I, lately, was not seeing Uncle Nasseem on a regular basis since he resided in New York while I live in New Jersey and I have a busy work schedule and family commitments. Our way of communication was basically occasional phone calls. I have noticed him to be forgetful and since May of 2013 things have gotten worse.
I have received several phone calls from him asking me his phone number because he realized that he didn't remember when he was asked for it..

I received phone calls from him asking me about the date and got confused if I told him that we were in a different month than what he thought.

I visited him in June 2013 with my oldest son. At that time he was so confused about how many kids I had; although a year before he would call and ask about my two sons by their names.

He became unable to take care of his usual needs. When I visited him in June of 2013, I took him to the local Laundromat since he had not washed his clothes for about three or four months.

I received a call from him asking me how to get to his barber shop that he had been going to for the last 15 years and over the phone I tried to give him the directions using MapQuest although I am not familiar with his area. I later found out that he never went to the barber until his sister-in-law took him about two months later.

I received a call from him complaining that he had a problem trying to pay his cable bill over the phone and when I called the cable company, they informed me that there were outstanding bills that he never paid.

When I told him that he has been forgetful and should not drive and use cabs instead, he told me that for some reason he feels nervous on the road but will work on this and try to get back to driving as he used to.

I have gotten calls from him saying that he just realized that he did not have food at home although every time I called him, I asked him to try to get a cab and buy enough food to last for some time.

Other than my experience with his confusion, Debbie, his sister-in-law (the elderly widow of his late half-brother) who lives in New York about 30 miles away, shared with me many issues related to his confusion and she tried to help him many times but she herself has health issues and was becoming concerned that she can no longer help him. She shared with me that:

She got a call from someone in a supermarket that noticed that Uncle Nasseem was confused and all he could respond with was Debbie's phone number.

She was trying to visit him weekly to help him go over his mail and help write checks for his bills.

She realized that he has been confused about his financial responsibilities. She mentioned that she knew that he would somehow get to the bank and withdraw his SS money not realizing that he needed to have the money in the account since he was writing checks. He would also be looking at the mail and would not able to differentiate between an advertisement and a bill. She told me that when she was with him one time, he had in front of him a coupon for oil change and she had to stop him from writing a check with the amount of the coupon.

She received a call from a woman who found him standing next to his car on the expressway and stopped to ask him if he needed help but he was confused and the only thing he gave her was Debbie's phone number. The police were called and eventually the police gave him a ride to Debbie's house.

She went shopping with him prior to going on a three-week trip to visit her son. She called me and told me that he should be okay with his food supply until I visit him a week later (which we have planned on since she was going away).

She also told me that lately many times during his confusion, he tried to communicate with her in Arabic, which she did not understand.

The final event was that I received a call from my cousin (Debbie's son) informing me that his brother got a call that Uncle Nasseem is in the hospital. Although I tried to understand how he was brought to the hospital, I was not able to get details other than that the police found him and he was brought in an ambulance to the Emergency Room and was then admitted. This occurred around 9/19/2013. When I visited Uncle Nasseem at the hospital, he told me that he was driving his car on the highway trying to get to the mall when he realized that he missed the exit. He said that he decided to make a U turn but the cars were going very fast so he remained on the shoulder waiting for two hours and then found several police cars coming toward him and then an ambulance.

At the hospital, the medical team decided that he should only be released with someone taking responsibility of him or to a nursing home. I am Uncle Nasseem's closest relative, but I am not capable of observing him around the clock. I therefore requested from the hospital's social worker to arrange for him to be transferred to a nursing home closer to me in New Jersey. He was transferred to NJ on 10/11/2013. I visited him on the same day to bring him some clothing items that he might need until somebody was able to bring him whatever he needs from his apartment. So far, I think that he is not accepting the fact that he needs help and he feels abandoned by his family.

My Relationship with Uncle Nasseem:

In Egypt, when I was growing up, Uncle Nasseem used to visit us, take me and my siblings out for dinner or ice-cream, babysit for my mother etc.

Uncle Nasseem immigrated to the United States when I was around 12 years old and I remember the whole family going to the airport to say goodbye. We kept in touch through letters in which I always updated him on how I am doing in my studies and exams. After few years, he started to visit Egypt during his vacation every 2–3 years and I got to see him each time he came. In 1991, after I completed medical school, I came to this country and I started my medical training in New York in 1992. I was seeing him on a regular basis for about four years until I went to DC to complete my training for another three years. He came to my wedding in 1999. When I had an employment opportunity, I went back to NY in 2000 with my wife and my son. We stayed there for three years and we were seeing uncle on a regular basis. My family and I had to make another move to southern NJ in 2003 and once again I was communicating with Uncle Nasseem over the phone. We were able to meet in person on couple of occasions; my cousin's wedding and my other uncle's funeral. I visited

Uncle Nasseem twice in 2005 to help him while he was moving from one apartment to another which happened at a time that we were mourning the loss of my other uncle (his brother) in Egypt. We always talked about him visiting southern NJ until he finally made the trip in 2007 few months before my youngest son was born. The next time we met was in Egypt in 2011 when I went for my mother's funeral. We always kept in touch by phone. He tried to learn to use emails but was never able to communicate well with them, so we gave up on the email idea.

Relatives for Mr. Aziz in this country:
Amir Ishak (nephew) (son of the late biological sister), Debbie Aziz (sister-in-law) (wife of late half-brother), Thomas Aziz (nephew / son of the late half-brother)"

"You didn't choose me, neither I chose you but for some reason I am asking to be your guardian. I am anxiously waiting for the court proceedings not knowing what will happen. I filled out the paper work with the attorney, he said it should take 45–60 days, and it has been about a month with no news. I have this fear that when the attorney assigned by the court comes to you in the nursing home, you will be so upset to hear about it. I don't even know if he/she will tell you directly that I filed with an attorney to become your guardian. I am also nervously waiting to hear from the Medicaid office about your application. I have no plan B if you are not approved for the coverage. Have no idea what I would do! Your nursing home asked for $12,000/month

and they already got from Debbie $24,000. She is hoping that when your Medicaid is approved, she will get her money back. I am in my fifties and my youngest child is six years old and yet I feel that I just had another one who is 74. It's sad to say that I can have a real conversation with my six years old but with you I feel that it is impossible to talk to you. If you were my dad, it would have been different but then my dad had almost your same problem and I wasn't there to be his "guardian," I hope you can just stay calm until I get the hang of this guardianship thing if you even allow me to."

These were the thoughts that were on Amir's mind that December of 2013 every time he walked through the doors of the Sunshine Rehab Center. Walking in the hallways, he would close his eyes and hope that Uncle Nasseem was *okay.* He always tried to calm himself, *If something had happened, they would have called, after all I am the only one, they contact.* In fact, despite that there was a couple of people that were sharing with him the burden of the deterioration of his uncle's mental abilities, he felt that ultimately, he was responsible of taking care of him since the day he told him that he was going to pick him up from the hospital and take him home. Now, Amir remembered again that he needed some help and support from the church. He contacted Father George, who was the priest in the Coptic Orthodox church in Sewell, NJ and asked him to visit Uncle Nasseem and from time to time, give him communion.

Chapter Five
"Where is the Car?"

When Amir attempted to ask Uncle Nasseem at the hospital about what exactly happened that led him in the hospital, he couldn't get a full answer. "I was in the car on Sunrise Highway trying to get to the mall, but I missed the exit, so I tried to make a U-turn on the highway. The cars were coming around me very fast. I stayed in the car for two hours, but I couldn't make the U-turn. I then found about ten police cars around me then they brought me here."

This was by far the longest answer he could get from Uncle Nasseem for a long time and was the last answer that made some sense to Amir. It didn't make sense to him that there were many police cars surrounding his car. He wished he knew what the police officers were suspecting when they saw a car stopped in the middle of one of the busiest highways on Long Island with a driver inside trying to make a U-turn. For one thing, Amir knew that Sunrise Mall was one of his favorite malls that he visited thousands of times and not being able to go there was adding to the picture that just having him alive after this incident was a miracle.

"What is going to happen to Nasseem when he gets older and needs help? Who is going to be around to help him?" These were the questions that Amir used to think

about. The answer to these questions was becoming clearer everyday. It was Amir that would be the one watching and arranging the care.

Then came the question, where is the car now? How can he find it? During what was happening, this was the last thing on Amir's mind. He started to wonder about it after Nasseem was finally transferred to the Nursing center in NJ. It wasn't something that Amir was interested in finding out but while he was working on the Medicaid papers, the question about Nasseem's assets came up, and he had to try to find out the answer to the question. In the Medicaid papers, he had to sign a paper that he will try to find the car and sell it within six months. To start with, he went to the police station in his town and reported that the car was missing. The police officer took all the information from him and told him to come back in few days to get the report.

Amir's previous experience with the police department in his town was that they were very laid-back. Surprisingly, with all what is happening in the world and in our country from terrorist attacks to school shootings, you can still find police departments that don't seem to be on edge. This could be a nice balance that allows the people living in the community to have the same attitude and not be nervous in all aspects of their lives.

One day Amir's son, Johnathan was going out for the school bus early in the morning as his high-school had an additional early class. His bus stop was down the hill from their house and Amir was watching him from the dining room window going out from the garage to the drive way. As he was walking in the driveway in the dark, a car was going on the street up the hill and stopped just after it passed their driveway. A tall man came out of the car and was putting on gloves. It was still dark and Amir could not see what the man looked like. Amir ran to the door, called out for Johnathan as he had run back into the garage, and closed the garage door. Amir went back to look from the window and the man, and the car were gone. Johnathan then opened the garage door and went back to go to his bus stop while Amir was watching him until he got on the bus and texted him his usual text, *On the bus*. Amir then called the police and told them the story. A police officer came to the front door and to Amir's surprise was not impressed with his story. He said that it was a quiet neighborhood and they had not received any issues and asked Amir to let them know if there were any other incidents. Amir remained nervous for few days until he realized that the man who came out of the car and was putting on his glove was the new newspaper delivery guy, so his worries were not warranted. The problem was that the man never attempted to greet Johnathan or to make his moves less dramatic, which got Amir and Johnathan concerned.

Amir knew that the police may not be helpful in finding the car but he needed to have a report so he could submit to Medicaid. He started to make phone calls to different police stations on Long Island to try to find where they towed the cars to. He also thought that if the car was towed to a facility, they might end up asking for storage fees which may even exceed the value of the car. He searched the internet, called different places; one place would give him a number to another, all with no luck. When Amir gave up looking, he decided to go back to the police station to pick up the report. It was a different officer on duty different from the one that talked to Amir and told him to come back in few days to pick up the report. It turned out that the first officer never filed a report or even made any note of it, so Amir needed to state his whole story again to the new officer. This officer seemed to Amir to be more mature and he told Amir, "Let me try to track the car first for you before filing a report."

After he took the information, he asked Amir to wait and in just a few minutes he came back to Amir and said, "I found the car for you. It was towed to a parking lot in Long Island and he gave him the information."

Trying to release the car from that place was not an easy job. At that time, Amir still did not have any authority to do anything on Uncle Nasseem's behalf. Now he was in the nursing facility, still confused of what was happening to him. The person who answered the phone when Amir called to inquire about the car understood the circumstances but still asked him to get something written from Mr. Aziz, allowing the car to be released to someone else. Amir could not be the one getting the car. He didn't have the time to take public transportation, get to Long Island, then drive the car back to NJ and, where was he going to put it? Debbie lived closer to that place and she was not only willing to take the car but in fact, understandably, wanted to do so, so that the car can be a partial repayment for the money that she paid to the nursing facility. Amir welcomed her eagerness, but he had to do the work.

He stopped by the nursing home carrying the paper for him to sign. He also needed to have them notarize it for him. He didn't know what Nasseem's reaction will be when he reads the paper. By then, Nasseem had already started to lose so much from his ability to comprehend written words.

"They found the car," Amir said to him in a positive tone.

"That's good news," Nasseem responded going along with Amir's happy tone.

"Now you have to sign this so Debbie can go and pick it up."

Amir let him read it over and over while he was realizing that he couldn't understand it. It was even tougher to ask him to sign a check so that Debbie can pay the storage money for the car. After repeating and repeating, he finally signed the check and the release paper. He also signed a statement that Amir wrote on his behalf that Debbie Aziz will be the one to get it. The administrator in the center helped Amir by notarizing the paper. Debbie got the car back and was able to negotiate the storage fees to half the amount they originally asked for. Amir felt better that the check he signed was made out to Debbie. The car remained with Debbie and became hers.

Chapter Six
The Big Important Things!

Although Amir's interest in medicine should have sparked an interest in exploring more about dementia and how to deal with it, the fact that he knew, as well as anybody else in the world, that there is no cure to it made him less enthusiastic about exploring. Every now and then, you hear about some medication being introduced to the management but there is yet to be a breakthrough for treating this disease. When Amir's primary care doctor knew that his late father and his uncle got it, she encouraged him to stay active since research showed that people who remain mentally active have slower progression of the disease. She was even very alarmed when Amir had a brain MRI that showed "atrophic changes" and asked him to see a neurologist. The MRI itself was done as part of evaluation for vertigo that Amir suffered from for a long time. The Neurologist assured him that these are normal findings that occur with age, but his family doctor remained skeptical.

From the little readings that he read, he learned that the victims of this disease suffer different kinds of problems with different rate of progression. Amazingly enough, some of the dementia sufferers can concentrate enough to record their problems and even write books about it. It seems that the support system that the patient has makes a big difference in the progression of the disease and that is why the dementia manifests itself differently. As for Uncle Nasseem, he had many disadvantages that aided in making his disease take a 'rapid' course. Nasseem lived by himself for a long time. After he was laid-off from his last job, his interaction with the outside world became very minimal.

Nasseem surrendered to the fact that he retired and was living off of his social security income. Amir didn't know exactly when he left his last job, but it must have been around 2004. He was keen on going to Egypt at least once a year to visit his older brother. Since his brother was also single and never married, they enjoyed having some time off together going to one of the Red Sea resorts in Egypt. Even though he had left his job, he never extended the time that he would spend in Egypt as if he was being careful not to abuse his brother's hospitality. Nasseem's brother was only a couple of years older than him, but Nasseem always acted like the youngest who always needed advice from his older brother.

In 2005, he got the news that his brother passed away suddenly in Egypt and he called Amir to tell him. It happened at a time when Nasseem's landlord had asked him to find another apartment since she was selling the family house that he rented an upstairs apartment in for more than ten years. He had found an apartment in a government subsidized building which meant a great break in the rent and he was getting ready to move. When he called Amir to tell him that Uncle Karim passed away, Amir felt bad that he would be sitting by himself and drove over to New York to be with him while he was mourning. When he got there, he found out that he was supposed to be preparing to move and he had not packed any of his stuff yet. This did not alarm Amir since he always knew that Uncle Nasseem almost always did everything at the last minute. Amir couldn't stay long this time because he realized that he needed to come back later and help him on the day prior to the move and help him while the movers were working.

When he went there few days later, it seemed like he had done no additional packing. Amir spent the night packing so that when the movers came in the morning, they had boxes to move. Nasseem was not happy with Amir's pace and thought that he was rushing him. He did not let him throw away anything that he had kept for many years. After Amir found out that Nasseem wasn't letting go of anything, he started packing everything. He told him that after he moved, he needed to go through the boxes and get rid of the things that he didn't need. Six years later, when he was at the hospital and Amir went to his apartment, he found all the boxes that he had packed not even touched.

Nasseem's brother's death seemed like an open invitation for him to spend more time in Egypt. The following years he would go there and spend 5–6 months during the winter from November to April or May. In Egypt he would stay in the apartment, go out shopping for necessities, then back to the apartment. The only contact with people he would have was with old friends, whom he would call and rarely meet. He was not interested that much in visiting his sister, Amir's mother, who was not in good health at that time since he had never liked being around sick people. He would only pay her one visit at Christmas. He would take the two-and-a-half-hour train ride from

Cairo to Alexandria and stay there for a couple of hours then head back to Cairo on the train to go to the apartment.

Amir's mother passed away in December of 2011 and Nasseem was in Cairo. He missed her funeral and went to Alexandria on the same day that Amir arrived from the US. It was the first time he had seen Amir after he had helped him with his move. He left to Cairo just few minutes after Amir's arrival and later he went back to the US in May. His next (and last) trip to Egypt as Amir expected was going to be in November.

Surely enough, he planned on going to Egypt in November of 2012 and he called Amir to tell him that he was going. To Amir's surprise, that time, he told Amir the exact date that he was traveling on. For all the years that Nasseem had been going to Egypt, he would never tell anyone when exactly he was leaving. He sometimes was afraid that Amir would ask him to carry something with him for his mother. It was true that every now and then Amir did ask him to carry something that he thought his mother needed. That year, Nasseem kept telling Amir on the phone that he was going to leave on November 4. That happened to also be his birthday and he kept saying that he was leaving on his birthday. He also called Amir's sister, Mona, in Egypt and told her that he will be travelling on his birthday. Whether they should have noticed that this was out of character for Nasseem and that they should have noticed that he was starting to show signs of needing help, who knows?

In Amir's reading about Alzheimer's, he was interested in finding a book or article about how people who lived by themselves were first discovered to have Alzheimer's and by whom were they discovered but he didn't come across any. Looking back, he became increasingly certain that Uncle Nasseem's problems had started at least sometime in 2012 but he was able to conceal it for a long time. He managed to travel across the Atlantic Ocean and to communicate with two different languages during the time that he was starting to lose control of his memory. There must have been incidents along the way that people would ask him a question or ask him about his travel documents and not get a direct answer from him and they would find the answer in the papers he was holding in his hand.

It had to be that he trained his brain to concentrate on the most important thing for the moment and try to avoid any distraction until he got that most important thing done. Once this was achieved, he could let go from stressing his brain for a while until the next most important thing came. It was not hard for him to ask some cab or limo to take him to his apartment in Cairo because he didn't have to stress his brain to remember an address that is imbedded in his memory. How did he pay the driver? That was another issue that nobody could answer other than Nasseem and the driver. Moreover, if Nasseem now couldn't answer this question, then the driver must have been the winner of some extra US Dollars instead of Egyptian pounds. These things remained unnoticed since nobody was watching.

While he was staying in his apartment in Cairo during his last trip, Nassem's activity did not cause anybody to suspect that there was something wrong. The cleaning lady that used to stop by when he visited came and helped him with his grocery and his needs. How did he pay her? Or how he managed to go to the bank to get or exchange money?

No one knew. The last trip, however, was a little different in the fact that this was the only trip that he called his niece, Mona, who lived in another city in Egypt to ask her to send one of her grown up kids to him, but he would not tell her the reason. There was something also strange that Mona told Amir that had happened, and she could not figure out what it was.

Mona told Amir that the cleaning lady called her to tell her that Nasseem once called her and was very disturbed. He told her that some people called him and threatened him that they will kick him out of the apartment and that he should just leave. When Mona called Nasseem to find out what had happened, he gave her no answer and told her that he did not know what she was referring to. Delusions sometimes are part of the manifestation of Alzheimer, but Mona and Amir were not alerted by this. His stay in Egypt otherwise went by unnoticed by anyone since he was able to get what he needed to stay alive. "The next big thing" for him was to take the plane back to New York and it turned out that a friend of his without noticing all the changes in Nasseem's condition helped him arrange that. He arrived in New York in May of 2013 and then many things happened to him that led him to the Sunshine Rehab center in NJ.

The early days after he came to NJ were not that bad. After moving from one room to another and eventually getting a private room and, most importantly, with a private bathroom, Nasseem seemed to be managing okay. It was either that something from what Amir told him worked or that his mental abilities were worsening, and his behavior had changed.

In the beginning he had Amir's phone number on a piece of paper and managed to call Amir several times. Amir, at first, had mixed feelings about the phone calls. In a sense, they at least let him know that he was okay but many times in the beginning, he got calls that were very disturbing. Just few days after he arrived, he called him and told him that he must leave, and Amir had to come to take him home. In his mind, Amir knew he was not capable of taking care of himself and the best thing for him was to have people to provide him with the care and food that he needed. Although, Amir believed in that, Nasseem's initial behavior made some of the staff believe that Amir should really come and take him. He got a call from an administrator in-training at the center telling him that Nasseem should leave because he was not happy. Every time he met him he complained that he wanted to leave.

When Amir met this administrator at the center and talked with him and told him about all Nasseem's problems he still did not believe that Amir didn't have any other better solution for his uncle other than being in that place. That time when Amir went to Nasseem's room, he found that Nasseem had some of his clothes out on a chair and when he saw him, he said that he had to leave and if Amir did not take him, he will get "the manager" to take him home. When Amir asked where home was, he told him that the manager promised him that he will take him in his car to his apartment in Cairo. Amir had to use the Medicaid ticket that was able to get him out of several situations like this. Often, he would say, "Uncle Nasseem, you just have to consider that you are in a not so nice hotel until the Medicaid is approved because they are asking for a lot of money." He once answered that he had money in Egypt which Amir knew that he had some money but not enough to cover the cost of even ten days in the center. Waiting for Medicaid to be approved was usually a successful answer.

Amir also tried reaching out to the social worker at the center. He told her once that Nasseem would probably like it if someone smiled at him or complemented his hair. He thought that this might work in situations when he was complaining and wanted to leave. When she met Amir, the next time, she told him that his advice worked. She said, "As soon as I complemented him on his hair, his eyes wide opened and was more receptive to anything I said."

The Medicaid process along with the guardianship took several steps. For the guardianship, Amir wrote the letter to the attorney explaining why he should be Nasseem's guardian and he submitted the case. The Attorney told him it usually took about two months. In the meantime, he needed him to arrange two evaluations by two physicians saying that he was mentally incapacitated. Gina at the nursing center gave Amir a list of physicians and he contacted a few until he found two that agreed to go to the center to evaluate him. He had to pay them out of pocket $1,100 for their service. Amir was not sure if they would be able to realize that his mental abilities were severely diminished. Amir knew Uncle Nasseem for years and he knew that he had lost so much of his mental power. He tried to convince himself that they were professional people and should be able to realize it. Not being familiar with adult medicine, he did not know that there were some standardized tests to evaluate people in Nasseem's condition. He also tried to tell Nasseem that there will be some people coming to ask him questions and he should just be nice to them and answer them. The common comment in their report was that he was not cooperating with them but they both agreed on the fact that he was mentally incapacitated. In a sense, Amir was relieved that someone else agreed with him that he needed help and supervision.

As the guardianship process was going on, it turned out that the normal procedure was that the court appoints an attorney (whose fees Amir had to also pay). The court-appointed attorney needed to visit Uncle Nasseem and determine that Amir would be the right guardian for him. Amir was in a meeting when he got a call from the attorney that visited the center and he couldn't answer the call. As soon as the meeting ended, and he was able to look at his phone, there was a voice mail:

"Hi Mr. Ishak, this is Stephanie Morris and I am here with your uncle and I wanted to talk to you" If you please give me a call on my cell phone…"

Standing in the Lobby of a high rise building in Philadelphia where his meeting was, he dialed the number that she left him.

"This is Amir Ishak, you left me a message."

"Thank you so much for calling back, I was sitting with your uncle, and I was hoping that you could help me talk to him since he was not really willing to talk to me."

"I'm sorry I was in a meeting."

"That's alright, I finally got him to talk to me and I asked him if he knows you and if he trusts you and he said yes. I also talked to the staff at the center and they also felt that you should be the guardian. I will submit my report to the court."

"Thank you."

"It will just take a few days until they receive it."

"Okay. Thanks again – have a good day!"

This was enough to make Amir feel that at least this part will be okay. He was disappointed few days later when his attorney called him to tell him that he had to appear in court on February 26.

"Didn't you tell me that it is a straightforward procedure and I don't have to appear in court," Amir answered him on the phone trying to hide his distressed voice.

"I know Mr. Ishak, but this judge is scrupulous, and she likes to see the guardian in person in her court."

"Okay, I will have to make adjustment in my schedule, and I will be there on the 26th."

"I'll meet you that day, it shouldn't take long."

The Medicaid application was taking longer than expected and Amir was getting nervous. He started receiving bills from the center for the charges after the money that Debbie put down ran out. His frustration got even worse when he kept calling the Medicaid office and left many messages to the case worker that was handling his application, to find out later that she had moved to another department and someone else was handling the application. After he talked to the new person handling the application, it took only few days for him to receive the approval for Medicaid. This approval was a great relief for Amir since it meant expenses were going to be covered. They, however, did not make it easy on him. Nasseem was admitted to the center in October, and Debbie had paid them the requested $24,000, which was supposed to cover two months of his stay, which meant that she had paid till December. The approval came effective January. That meant that the expenses from December to January needed to be paid. Amir got an email from Gina congratulating him on getting the Medicaid coverage. When he replied, asking about the period from December to January, she advised him to appeal.

As if it was not enough for Amir to gather everything for the initial application, now he had to appeal and fight for the uncovered time. Gina said to him that if he informed the center that he was appealing for the uncovered period they will wait to see the outcome of the appeal and thankfully, they did. It took until August for the Medicaid to respond granting coverage from December to January. Luckily, Debbie was not expecting to get her money back, otherwise that would have been another fight to try to get approval from the time he was admitted to the center which Amir was sure would not have been approved anyway.

Amir had to deliver the papers from the attorney indicating that he submitted papers for guardianship and there will be a court hearing. This was a routine legal procedure that his attorney told him had to be done. He also needed to confirm to the attorney that he delivered the papers to Nasseem. In the papers it indicated that if Nasseem had opposition, he should contact the attorney. Amir did not know how to explain the guardianship process to Nasseem. He was not sure how to word it in a way that did not hurt Nasseem's feelings and at the same time explain it honestly. All he said was, "I am putting these papers here; these papers are saying that you are allowing me to help you." He then felt he needed to elaborate a little more, "To help you with applying for the Medicaid and represent you until you feel better and are able to do things by yourself."

Nasseem's ability to understand long statements had been diminishing at that time so his response was something like repeating the statement with a question, he replied, "Help me? For how long?"

Amir felt that Nasseem's response meant that he did not get the part that he said, "Until you are able to do so," or maybe, nothing made sense to him altogether. He felt that he needed to answer but did not know what to say and without thinking, he just said, "Until I die."

As much as Amir regretted his sarcastic response, he felt that this could be true. Debbie's comment that she had made several times, "Nasseem is going to outlive us all by the way he takes care of his health," always resonated in his head. Amir was able to distract him again with the DVD player that he got for him to be able to watch some of his favorite black and white Arabic movies. As expected, this also did not go well. Just turning the power on and off was a major problem for Nasseem.

While Amir was trying to get Uncle Nasseem to concentrate, his room door was suddenly pushed open and a fellow patient in the nursing home came into the room with a threatening look. He had behavioral problems and his aide was not fast enough to prevent him from entering Nasseem's room. Amir, with his calm nature tried to nicely stop that man who just kept walking. Nasseem on the other hand did better than Amir in trying to defend himself. He walked toward the guy who turned around heading to the door.

Nasseem kept shouting, "I'll kill you!"

The day of the court appearance came. This was the first time for Amir to go to a court. After the security check and entering the building, he found himself in a hallway in front of three rooms with closed doors and few people in the hallway. There was a guard in front of every closed door, and he found the room that he was supposed to go in but he was about half hour earlier than the scheduled time. The guard told him that he could go in and sit in the courtroom until his case started. He went in and took the first bench he found and sat down quietly.

The first case was a person being sworn in to become like a monitor for guardians. The next case was another guardianship case, just like Amir's. This was a lady that was asking to be a guardian for her husband who had dementia. Amir was listening carefully when he got a text from the attorney. He had texted him earlier to let him know that he arrived and will go inside the room. The attorney was replying that he would meet him in the courtroom. Amir continued to listen to the attorney that came with the lady and then the lady's testimony. It turned out that she was the caregiver for her husband, and she needed to become guardian so she can start using his social security and pension money to take care of him. He did not qualify for Medicaid since his social security and pension were about $3,000 and that was above the limit. That meant that she could not afford to have him in a skilled nursing facility. Amir thanked God that his Medicaid problem was resolved. When that case was over, it was time for his case.

After he was sworn in by the clerk, the attorney started presenting the case.

Then the judge put a call to the court's attorney who had visited Nasseem in the center and talked to Amir on the phone a while back. That attorney on the phone told the judge that from her meeting with Mr. Aziz and the staff at the center, she recommended that Mr. Amir Ishak became his guardian. The judge had to ask Amir some questions and of course he could not help it and became emotional at some point while he was answering. The judge then closed the case by granting Amir guardianship and the authority to manage Nasseem's assets within $10,000. The condition to that was that if it were found out later that he had other properties or assets Amir had to go back to the court. Out of the courtroom, Amir went with his attorney to the surrogate's office to get the documents then had to leave to go to work.

Since Amir was receiving mail forwarded from Nasseem's older address, he was able to keep track of what needed to be done. He cancelled the phone service, cancelled the cable account. The forwarded mail started to fade, until one day he received a letter addressed to Nasseem. *Who sends letters anymore these days?* Amir wondered. The return address showed a name that was not familiar to him and since he was granted guardianship, he felt that it was okay for him to open the envelope. It was from a woman named Bonnie Smith.

Amir knew that although Uncle Nasseem lived by himself and had limited contact with people he had relationship with people that he worked with or was friends with. Before he started to lose his memory and Amir would ask him about who took care of paying his rent and other stuff when he traveled to Egypt and stayed there for six months, he would only say "some friends." It turned out that Bonnie, who lived in Texas, was someone who he had trusted to do so. The letter from Bonnie was saying that she had not been able to reach him, and she wanted to check on him but the phone number that she had for him was disconnected. She wrote him her phone number. Amir sensed from her letter that she was someone that was a genuine friend and he gave her a call. It was around ten o'clock in the morning when Amir called Bonnie and did not realize the time difference between the eastern and central time until the voice on the other end sounded like someone who just woke up. Amir apologized to her and tried to make it short by just telling her that Uncle Nasseem is now in a nursing home in NJ and that he had dementia. Bonnie did not seem to be bothered by the early phone call and sounded to Amir as if she wanted to prolong the conversation for a little more.

She told Amir that she had known Nasseem for about thirty years. She got to know him first when he was working in his first job when he came to this country. She was a secretary in the hospital that he worked at as a patient transport tech. When he started working on his masters, he needed her help to type reports. At that time, she had left the hospital, so he bought a typewriter and took it to her house to type the reports. She told Amir that he used to pay her and buy her gifts in appreciation for her work. Amir pretended that he did not know Nasseem very well when she was saying, "Nasseem was always late in his reports and he would bring some hand-written papers to me late at night and ask me to have them ready early in the morning to meet a deadline." Many times, she had to stay up late and have her husband take care of her kids until she was done with Nasseem's papers. She said that the only thing that Nasseem was never late for was picking up the papers the next day.

She told Amir that although she had moved to Texas with her family years ago, Nasseem kept in touch and he always asked her to help him when he traveled for extended time. She said that he would send her checks dated for rent and ask her to send it on time. She knew that every time he came back, he changed his phone number and she waited for him to call her. When he had not called for long time after she expected him to be back, she decided to send the letter. When she learned about his deteriorating dementia, she said to Amir that she always wondered what would happen to him, as he grew older. She knew that the social isolation he was in was not going to be good for him and she asked Amir to convey to him her best wishes.

Chapter Seven
To Learn or Not to Learn?

Amir did not have a doubt that he needed to educate himself more about this mysterious disease. As mysterious as it is there is nothing mysterious about the treatment. There is simply no cure yet and that's why he was facing a big question, "Why bother?" Ideally when he faced a medical problem, he searched and researched but, in this situation, he just did not feel like knowing what exactly happens inside the brain yet. He convinced himself that if he heard about a breakthrough, he will be open to listening more about how it can cure this disease. Yet, a part in him that wanted to learn was surfacing from time to time. He wanted to be prepared for that breakthrough. In addition, it was on his mind that in the future, he might face this same problem, but still, he thought, he probably will then not be able to comprehend at that time that there is something wrong with him.

His mom took care of his dad when he started to have memory problems, Amir was thousands of miles away, so he did not know the details. She traveled with his dad these thousands of miles while Amir was still in his medical training in the US just to give Amir an idea on what was going on. They stayed with him at his one-bedroom apartment in a high-rise building close to his work. What Amir observed of his dad at that time was that with his memory issues, he became very quiet. He suddenly became so obedient to Amir's mom; sat where she wanted him to sit; ate what she wanted him to eat even if it was something that he would never have liked before. They stayed with Amir for a month, but it was enough for Amir to see how this disease could affect a person so bad that you just let go and let people handle you. He didn't think that being dependent on others bothered his dad as much as it bothered his mom, physically and emotionally.

After they left and went back to Egypt, things started to slowly deteriorate. Luckily, his dad did not have medical problems, but Amir's mom had to deal with some behavioral issues that came at one of the stages of the disease. In his dad's case, as Amir recalled it, was not that bad, but it might have been embarrassing to his mother in front of some of their neighbors. After about thirteen months, his mom was able to wisely make the decision that she did not have to send him to the hospital when family members and some doctors suggested putting a feeding tube. He comfortably passed and Amir couldn't be there for the funeral. His mom visited him a few months later and she brought back in her suitcase the medicine that he had read about and sent it to them in case it could be of help.

At times, Amir believed that he had an obligation, at least, to read a little bit about Alzheimer/Dementia. Debbie recommended to him to read a book called "*Learning to speak Alzheimer* which he enjoyed. He also read *Living in the Labyrinth* and *Still Alice*. That of course in addition to several *google* searches.

He remained in a state of distraction by what was happening and what he felt he needed to do for Nasseem. With many things on his mind, he was going to the bank one morning to deposit some checks. Although he usually preferred to get out of the car over going through the drive through option, this time he wanted to stay in the car. His son was in the back seat and he didn't want him to get out in the freezing cold. He picked up the container that goes through the tube and put the checks in it then closed it, put it in the machine where it gets sucked up in the ducts to the teller. He waited until the teller returned the tube with the receipt in it. "Have a good day!" said the teller through the microphone and Amir responded. He looked at the receipt then without thinking turned around and handed the container to his son and started to pull out of the drive thru.

"Oh, we get to keep this?" said his son. Amir had developed a habit to not respond to his kids until they say what they wanted at least twice. "Dad, do we get to keep this?"

Amir turned around and could not stop laughing. "Of course not, it's a mistake," he replied. He had to go back to the bank to put the container back in the machine.

It is true what people say that the early signs of dementia are sometimes subtle for even the very close family to recognize it. Amir was so puzzled and worried in the very early days. He waited for Medicaid to be approved and the nursing home expenses to be taken care of. He also needed to prove that Nasseem did not have other income or assets and a medical report to confirm the diagnosis. Amir never had any knowledge of how physicians confirm the diagnosis just by a quick visit and assessment. In his mind he believed that there is no way that Uncle Nasseem could manage to live in a place by himself after what happened to him, but he wasn't sure if that was easy or hard to prove to others. To start with, his wife felt that he was making a big mistake when he was fighting to bring him from New York to New Jersey. The fact that the nursing home requested the $24,000 for the two months upfront also did not make it better. "What if Medicaid is not granted, who can afford the $12,000 monthly bill of the nursing home." She told Amir on the phone when he had just talked to Debbie as she had offered to pay the initial two months. "I don't agree with what you are doing."

He was at work and in his kind of work sometimes it is very hard to allow a little distraction from the care of the critically sick newborns that are in the NICU. Practically sometimes the babies are stable enough and he can be distracted a little bit while counting on the experienced nurses and the residents to come to him if there is any need. He always felt better to be sitting in the unit rather than going to his office which may be more private but was few Hallways away from his patients. He made a quick decision despite his wife's warnings. He was just focused on bringing Uncle Nasseem to New Jersey. Amir also remembered that at some point in the conversation she had suggested that if Nasseem just moved to an apartment close to them, they could check on him and make sure he was safe. Although Amir did not think that this could work, he kept it in his mind as a last resort.

When Nasseem came to NJ and was complaining that he wanted to go home which was a valid and reasonable complaint, Amir kept doubting himself thinking that Uncle

Nasseem could be right and he could be wrong. The greatest next challenge was how he can manage his finances until the Medicaid is approved when he didn't have any authority. For a person who is very conscious about not breaking any rules the challenge was even greater, but he had to come out of his comfort zone at certain times so that things work out well.

Some of the things he needed to do were easy to do with today's technology, others he had to be creative.

He needed to make sure that he received Nasseem's mail in NJ so he can respond and/or find out if there are any bills he needed to pay and/or cancel certain services. This was not hard, since now you can request forwarding the mail online and it can go up to six months.

He was able to cancel his TV/phone and internet services by a phone call.

He needed to make sure that the Social Security payments that Nasseem was getting were deposited in his account. He needed to somehow withdraw the money before a two months' period occurred to keep the balance below $2,000. Until he became the guardian, he could not withdraw any money unless it was a check that was signed by Nasseem. Amir was able to call the bank when he was visiting Nasseem and asked him to tell the clerk that he wanted to change the address. He was also able to come up with reasons for him to write checks for Amir so at least the balance would remain low. Although Amir knew that he needed this money for multiple reasons (continue to pay the rent for the apartment in NY until he was sure that he will remain in NJ, pay the expenses for the Guardianship process, keep the SS money since this is what will be his payment for the center, pay for the expenses that Debbie paid for the car when she retrieved it…etc.) he was not sure if what he was doing was entirely legal without him having a real authority.

Amir needed to feel that he had some documentation of what he was handling for Nasseem as if there will be a time that all Nasseem's memory and brain functions will come back and he will ask him about everything that he had done. There was no problem for Amir writing down exactly what checks he had him write, and what he paid, and he kept everything in an excel file (this continued on until the day that he did not need it anymore).

The problem with Nasseem's bank was that it was a local bank in NY and did not have branches in NJ. He called the bank and begged the clerk to change Nasseem's address but they would not do it since his name was not on the account. Despite this, the clerk hinted to Amir that he could sign him up for Online banking and then he could view the updated balance. Amir was able to do so and that helped him bypass this hurdle until he had legal authority to do so.

Being able to take videos with his phone was one of the things Amir did with the same thought in mind that one day he will question why he asked him to sign certain checks and where the money went. Amir did not do it all the times, but he did it when he could and because this technology was not something that Nasseem was familiar with, he did not notice or question Amir while he had his phone in his hand taking the videos.

When Amir finally got the court order that granted him to be his guardian, it was a great relief for him that he had a new document that allowed him to help.

During the time that he was waiting for the guardianship papers, he was paying for Nasseem's apartment in NY. He knew that the subsidized apartment was not easy for Nasseem to get and he was on a waiting list for a long time. Amir figured out how to submit the rent and managed for five months to either have him sign a check or paid with his own check and put it on his excel spreadsheet that Nasseem owed him that amount. As soon as he got the guardianship document, he contacted the bank to figure out how to close Nasseem's account and he spoke to the township where his rent went to tell them that he would terminate the lease.

Vacating the apartment was the next thing Amir needed to do. He arranged a visit to LI with Debbie so they can go over all what he had in the apartment. It was a very cold day in February, and he left NJ very early in the morning to get to Nasseem's apartment before the morning rush. When he arrived at the apartment, he immediately knew that it was not going to be an easy job. He had told his wife that it could take more than one day and if he needed, he, will go and spend the night at Debbie's house which was about twenty minutes from Nasseem's apartment. When he arrived there, Debbie had not yet arrived, and he started slowly looking into Nasseem's stuff. Debbie came about an hour later. Amir had not seen her since he attended his uncle's funeral about seven years before and was surprised to see how much weight she had lost. Evidently, she had been having GI troubles, just like Amir himself.

He left Debbie for a little while to go to the bank to close the account. The bank procedure was not as straight forward as he thought, and they needed some time. They told him that they will have to send him the check with the balance in the mail. He went back to Debbie in the apartment after he stopped by a place to pick up some food since they were going to spend the whole day in the apartment. Just as he expected, it took a long time to go over the papers, the clothes and the untouched boxes from the time that he moved into the apartment. Amir had started to feel that he was the one to make decisions and for that reason he was trashing as much of the stuff as he could if it seemed to him of no value or need. Amir recalled the time that he went and helped Uncle Nasseem move to this apartment. Nasseem did not want to throw any single item in his apartment and at that time Amir had to put everything in boxes for him regardless of what he thought about it. During that moving time, Amir convinced Nasseem to let go of some of his old books and magazines that he had when he was working for the insurance company. Since Nasseem only agreed at that time that his new apartment was too small to put all his boxes in, he gave Amir some of the boxes to put in his basement. Amir eventually went over the boxes in his basement and threw most of them and only kept a couple of books and a dictionary that he felt might be useful.

He was hoping that they will find some money that Nasseem had hidden somewhere in his apartment. Between Debbie and himself they had spent more than $30,000 in the last few months arranging things for Nasseem's care and it would have been nice if Nasseem had thought that at some point there will be a need for some cash for an emergency in the house. It turned out that there was no money in the apartment. Some of the things that they found were actually Debbie's documents in Arabic which Nasseem kept for her. Amir helped translate the documents for Debbie.

There were some items in the apartment that Amir and Debbie felt they would find some use for. He had a relatively new computer, the vacuum cleaner that Amir brought him when he visited with his son, some old Polaroid cameras that Amir felt he can show to the kids. Amir also kept some of the pictures that he found for Nasseem. When they were done around 8:00 pm, he loaded what he was taking in his car and what Debbie was taking in her car. They were not finally done until 9:00 pm and by then Amir was so tired and he just wanted to go home rather than spending the night and trying to go back in the morning when the traffic could be bad. Debbie told him that she would keep the keys since she wanted to stop by another time to make sure that they did not leave behind anything needed and then she was going to leave the key with the superintendent.

After the Medicaid was approved at the end of January 2014, Amir paid all the social security money that Nasseem received from the time he was admitted to the time Medicaid became effective to the rehab center. Moving forward, it was an easier process since Amir did not have to give the center any checks. The Medicaid took over his social security payment and it was accessible to the center without Amir's involvement. Until the time the Medicaid became effective, Amir never stopped worrying. He was worried that the Medicaid will be denied, that Nasseem will keep complaining and wanting to go home or he will suddenly get back his memory and want to go to his apartment in New York which he never mentioned at all at any time.

Amir was never completely satisfied with the care that Nasseem was getting in that nursing home. He felt that the people could have been a little friendlier or they could have tried harder to engage Nasseem in something that could have helped keep some of his mental abilities or at least made him "happier." He could not visit him often and was feeling bad that there is not much entertainment for him when he was not there. He brought from his house a VCR player and hooked it up to the TV that they had in the room for him. He also brought the tapes of the movies that he knew Nasseem liked and he was hoping that he would be able to play it sometimes or somebody will notice that he has the tapes and they would play it for him. He had a feeling that all the time that he was sitting in his apartment before the events happened, Nasseem was only playing his favorite movies over and over.

Watching old movies seemed to have been something that he just enjoyed. Whenever Amir tried to just have the TV on while he was there, it did not catch Nasseem's attention at all. Anything new was hard for him to grasp and just stressed him more. It was much easier for him to watch the movies that he had memorized; *Pretty woman*, *Coming to America* and *Working Girl* were his favorites. The most Amir was able to do for him at the center was that he would put a tape in the VCR and start one of the movies before he left and tried to draw Nasseem's attention to it then tell him that he would be leaving. He always wondered what happened after he left him. Amir knew some of the old Egyptian movies that Nasseem never forgot even after years of being in the US. He burnt some of them on CDs from YouTube, brought him a portable DVD player, and tried to explain to him how to work it. That did not work well at all. There was no way that he could remember how to turn it on. He ended with the same system; he would start the movie before he left and who knows what happens next!

On some of Amir's visits, he tried calling his sister in Egypt to have her hear Uncle Nasseem's voice. He would give him the phone when she answered and Nasseem would only say few words and mostly, "Yeh, yeh."

Chapter Eight
Out of Jail and Back!

For a while after Nasseem came to NJ, Amir feared the idea that they can try to go out together although he wanted him to at least get a breath of fresh air outside of the walls that surrounded him. All that Amir was trying to establish in Nasseem's mind was that this was where he lived, this was where his meals were and any care he needed was. This was not an easy task in the beginning. When he visited him on the first day of his arrival, they had put him in a room with a roommate. Amir knew right away that this will not go well with him. Amir came to him with some clothes that he went and bought until he was able to get some of his clothes from the apartment in LI.

On that first day, he seemed calmer than Amir thought. Then he remembered that when the social worker at the hospital called him and informed him that they had arranged the transport, he had suggested that she tells the medical team to give him something that will make him less agitated since he knew that he might give them a hard time. Amir was happily surprised that this first visit went well and when he went home and his wife asked how it went, he answered her, "It was better than I thought!"

Since it was not that bad of a start, Amir thought that he could make it even better for Nasseem. He went and bought a small Fridge and bought some grocery items to take with him the next time he visited. He called the priest of his church in NJ to let him know about Uncle Nasseem to put him on his list for people in the hospital to visit from time to time. Again, Father George said the same thing the priest in LI said, "Can't he stay home with you?" Amir continued to believe that he and his family did not have the time and ability to take care of Uncle Nasseem.

Having heard the comment that the nurse manager told him on the first time he visited, "You're in trouble; he said that you have a big house," Amir was feeling guilty that Nasseem might not really belong to a place like the one he was in. At the same time, Amir didn't think that there was any possibility that he can come and live with him. Even before all the troubles that he had, Uncle Nasseem was never a person that would be easy to live with. Growing up with his older brother, they always had conflicts that Amir witnessed when he was young, and he grew to understand that Nasseem had a unique personality that was great to get to know but sort of impossible to live with. Besides, the fact that there was no way that Amir's family could handle him at home while they were trying to take care of his two sons.

His older son was a teenager approaching his senior year in high school, with all what this entailed : Learning to drive; taking the SATs; applying for colleges and all the drama that surrounds all these events. Having grown up in a different country with different school system, this was an experience by itself that Amir had to go through and there was no place for Nasseem to be with them while they were trying to figure all this out. They also had their youngest son who was ten years younger and still needed all the attention.

Amir had always fought the thoughts that all these were just excuses they were trying to hold on to not to bring Nasseem into their lives. He believed that Nasseem needed a place where at least someone will be there all the time to watch him or, as they had in the center, the security band that alarms if he gets closer to a door.

Nasseem was admitted to the Sunshine Center in the middle of October and just after four weeks of being there, Thanksgiving was quickly approaching. Amir needed to put in Nasseem's mind that there was such a situation that they can leave the center together, go somewhere and then return to the center because the center was his place where he belonged. After moving from one room to the other and Nasseem got what he needed, a private room with private bathroom, Amir felt he could try to take him out. He was still visiting every few days and bringing some food and soda and he did not want to say anything about going out until the day he decided to take him to the mall. As he expected from the typical Uncle Nasseem, he needed time to dress up and comb his hair.

Amir was taking his mother-in-law to her apartment after she had visited them and he figured that on his way to her house, he would stop by the center, tell Uncle Nasseem to get dressed, and then take his mother-in-law, drop her off at her building and head back to the center. Although it took him more than forty-five minutes to return, Nasseem was still shaving his beard. Amir had to start guiding him through what he needed to do to get dressed. He stayed until he finished shaving and then showed him the clothes and stepped out of his room to give him a little bit of privacy which, knowing Nasseem, he liked. He kept going back in the room every few minutes until Nasseem was finally ready to put his pants on and it seemed like if Amir didn't help him, this would have taken another hour. Amir was surprised that Uncle Nasseem let him help put his pants, his socks then shoe on and they finally headed to the door.

Not so simple! He remembered his sunglasses. Nasseem always carried his sunglasses and his gloves in his hand, day and night. They were part of him and that's why Amir made sure to have them in his room but as expected, he would not know where they were. Luckily, Amir found them on one of the chairs and they walked out the door. At that time, he had gotten used to coming out of his room and walking the long hallway that took him to the farthest dining area that he liked better than the one closer to his room. Amir had gone to visit one time and one of the workers took him to where he was sitting having lunch. This time, he was walking out of his room in street clothes; something that he had not done in a while.

Nasseem loved to get attention – especially from the ladies. As they were walking down the hallways to reach the front door, they saw some of the aides who worked at the center. Amir knew that there were certain ones that he liked more than others. He first stopped at the nurses' station to announce that his nephew was there, and he was going out with him. People have started to know him, and everyone greeted him and complemented him on how nice he looked. This encouraged him to continue to get everyone's attention in the hallways to tell them that he was going out with his nephew.

As they walked out of the front door, Amir's heart was pounding. He did not know what to expect from him. In Amir's mind, he thought that this would be Nasseem's opportunity to tell him, "Now I got you! Take me home." It wasn't that long ago that Nasseem had repeatedly called him and told him that he needed to leave. Amir also did not forget the administrator in-training at the center that had called him once telling him that it seemed that it would be better for Nasseem to leave because he was not happy.

Nasseem acted very reasonable. He followed Amir's directions to walk until they got to where Amir had parked his car. Amir helped him get in the car which he knew was going to be a bit difficult with the SUV being high for his knees to bend.

They went to the mall and Amir was trying to put in his mind that he needed some clothes. He also repeatedly said to him that after they were done, they would be heading back to the center. At times, it seemed as if there was nothing wrong with Nasseem other than being Uncle Naseem, the stubborn, so hard to convince. He only stopped to look at the items that he always liked to buy. A pair of socks from Macy's was all he liked during this trip. He even insisted on paying. He still had some cash that Amir had left with him in the center since he wanted to have money. After the mall, they went to Burger King and he had a sandwich and at that time, Amir learned how he likes his Whopper (no pickles-no ketchup-no onions).

Amir could not be happier when he took him back to the center and instructed him to get out of the car, enter through the door and wait for him until he parked the car. It was a sigh of relief for Amir that Nasseem was at least accepting the fact that the Sunshine Rehab center was his place to return to.

This trip was followed by other trips. After a couple of visits and going out, Amir's visits to Nasseem somehow became linked in his mind with going out. When Amir would visit him with no intention to go out, he would look at him and say, "I thought we were going to go out?" Amir couldn't tell if his uncle was playing tricks like a child who wanted something from his father or if he had just linked it in his brain that Amir is the one that took him out.

After Amir took him out once for his favorite thing to do which was a haircut, it became all what he wanted to do. If Amir stops by one day just for a quick visit, he would say, "I thought, we were going to go out to have a haircut." He started clinging onto the thoughts that would make him feel that he can think and remember things.

Nasseem loved to keep a nice image of himself in front of people. He also loved to fix his hair and to be complemented on it. While they were going out one day Amir asked the front desk about having a haircut for him and they asked them to write a check and make an appointment. At that time, Nasseem used to have his check book while he was going out. Amir did not have the guardianship status approved yet and he had asked him to write checks for different things so that he can keep the account below $2,000, which was the maximum he was allowed to have in his account eligible Medicaid approval. He helped him write the check to the lady and they made the appointment. On the next visit, his hair was not cut, and Amir learned from the staff that he resisted to go to the second floor where the barber's room was located. Since

Nasseem really needed a haircut, Amir decided to just take him to Great Clips which is a barber shop chain that had one store not far from the center. Nasseem was so excited to go and was happy with his haircut and more so was happy with the beautiful lady that cut it. He asked her what her name was and had a small conversation with her. As much as Nasseem was satisfied with the haircut, Amir wasn't. He felt that it wasn't short enough to last for some time.

Now that Amir took him to the barber shop, he added a new task that became linked in Nasseem's mind that when they went out, he had to get a haircut. Two weeks later, Amir called the center and told them to tell Nasseem that he will be coming to pick him up to go out for a little bit. Amir had learned that he had to do this at least two hours before he planned on being there. Nasseem was expecting to get another haircut!

Then came Thanksgiving Day, Amir and his family had invited some friends from their church to a holiday dinner at their house.. The way the holidays are celebrated in the United States for immigrants such as Amir's family are very much different from the way the American's celebrate and different from how Amir's family celebrated back home in Egypt where he grew up. When Amir was growing up, the holidays were celebrated with family and extended family. Now being in the United States, in their church there were at least two kinds of families. The ones that were almost like Amir's family with at least one of the couple have their own parents back in Egypt and their kids are the first generation in this country. Then there were other families where the extended family of about two generations already in this country. For the first kind of families, the holidays became more like gathering with people that you know and not necessarily close family. In Amir's case, his wife had more family in this country than himself and during the holidays, when they had a gathering, they had friends from the church in addition to his wife's family. They used to invite their friends during Thanksgiving holiday and they, in return, invited them during other holidays. Thanksgiving was one of the unique holidays for most of the Egyptian families, especially the Christian ones like Amir's. Although it is not considered a religious holiday to the Coptic Christians, they almost made it like a religious holiday that deserves to be celebrated despite not having any similar holiday on the Coptic calendar.

Thanksgiving that year was different for Amir for the fact that he planned on having Uncle Nasseem with them. Amir was not sure how this would work. Nasseem did not know any of the people coming to Amir's house. He also had only seen Hoda, four times altogether with two of them only briefly. He had hardly met Amir's mother-in-law and his sister-in-law. As of Amir's kids, his oldest had visited him in his apartment few months back with Amir but Nasseem had never met the younger son who was six at that time. Amir still also was not so sure if Nasseem might react differently when he was supposed to take him back to the nursing home. By then he was only successful in going out with him for a couple of hours then going back to his room with no resistance. Amir did not know if being in a house would remind Nasseem that the normal way to live is in a house with some people you know.

When Amir went to the center, he found Nasseem, as usual, not ready to leave. He allowed Amir to help him put on his pants just to be able to save some time. They walked down the long hallways of the center and he had his jacket in his hand trying to attract anybody's attention to tell them that he is going to his nephew's house for dinner. Since Amir could not park his car just in front of the center's front door, he had to walk until they got to the car. This was not something different, since on their few trips that they made from the center together, they always walked to the car. Amir used to consider this a part of the trip, being out and free from the walls that surrounded him all the time. It was also good opportunity for Nasseem to walk and for them to talk about the weather. For Amir who walks fast, he had to take a deep breath and slow down. As soon as they got to the car, Amir unlocked the doors, and as he was opening the passenger side door for Nasseem, he stopped and turned to Amir signaling that he wanted to say something.

Amir was horrified and thought that Nasseem would ask if they were going to his apartment in Cairo, but he was a little relieved when he heard what he had to say. "Shouldn't we go get something to take with us?"

This was typical Uncle Nasseem, who wants to present himself in an admirable way. Amir told him that this was not necessary, and he could make it up another time.

During the twenty minutes ride to Amir's house, he tried to prepare him. He explained to Nasseem that when they get there, he will first meet Hoda, his wife, then his mother-in-law, his sister-in-law, his son Johnathan and his younger son Michael. He explained to him that there will be other people whom he did not know but they were from the church. Amir felt that, by saying "people from church" it was not going to be hard for him to comprehend since

Nasseem and his brother had always associated Amir with church. When Amir was growing up in Egypt, they used to tease him often that he always went to church and was involved in Sunday school and many church activities. It wasn't going to be strange for Nasseem to hear Amir talking about church.

Amir parked the car in the driveway and stopped the car so Uncle Nasseem can get out, then he wanted to pull the car out of the driveway to clear it for the other guests. Johnathan came out to help Nasseem until Amir parked the car on the street. Then Amir caught up with Uncle Naseem as he had just gotten into the house from the back door and was greeted by Amir's mother-in-law, his sister-in-law and his wife. They all led him to the family room.

Michael came to say "Hi" and Amir introduced him to Uncle Nasseem. Until then he appeared to everyone as normal as he could be. The only thing that was different was that he kept looking at Michael then turning to Johnathan and despite the ten years' difference and the size difference he kept asking who was older. Michael found that was very funny and could not help but laugh. This remained his main memory of Uncle Nasseem. Amir had downloaded several old Egyptian movies that he knew Nasseem would not mind watching and felt that they could use them if needed. When the people came and the environment seemed too confusing for Nasseem, Amir asked his son to play one of the movies on TV to entertain Nasseem instead of him sitting there just quiet. That worked for a while until the conversations became louder and he could not hear the TV. He suddenly turned to one of Amir's friends and said angrily, "You know, you should watch and listen to the movie." Amir had warned his guests a little that his uncle had some memory issues and that friend took it lightly and stopped talking for a little then the conversation went back to normal. Uncle Nasseem stood up and took a seat closer to the TV to be able to hear.

Nasseem joined everyone at the dinner table seeming normal and managed to eat what Hoda put in his plate with no problems. After they left the dinner table, Amir offered him dessert and he liked it. When Amir felt that it was about time to take him back, he told Nasseem that they should get going. There was no resistance. Amir's mother-in-law and his wife helped him find his coat and came to the door with them to say goodbye and he took him back to the center.

As much as Nasseem's acceptance to the new routine was making Amir feel better, he was still worried that there will be one time that Nasseem might insist on going home and refuse to accept that the center was his home. They had told Amir in the center that anytime Amir took him, he had to sign him out and in. Amir felt that putting this in his mind might be a safety cushion for Amir. He thought that if he told him, "Now I have to go to the office so they will let you come with me," this could remind him that the rules needed to be followed all the times. And when he brought him back he would tell him, Now I have to let them know that you are back". This trick worked, and Nasseem mostly went along with it.

As the staff became familiar with Amir and saw him several times, Amir could sense that not everyone was that strict about documenting the time he left and the time he came back. Nasseem also noticed that. When Amir would tell him, "Now, I have to stop by the nurse's office to sign you out," he would say, "No, you don't have to, they don't care." This made Amir start to worry again that Nasseem was still noticing things and that he was not completely "out of the woods" when it came to possible problems from Uncle Naseem.

Nasseem had a paper with Amir's name and phone number next to his bed and, in one of the first rooms that he had there was a working phone line. He would call at different times just to say hi or to say, "When are you coming?" He once called at six o'clock in the morning while Amir was getting ready to leave for work. When it turned out that he was just saying "Hi," Amir tried to tell him nicely that he probably needed to go back to sleep because it was too early in the morning.

Amir found out that trying to repeat and inform him what to expect as much as he could helped him to not appear confused or scared when they were out in public.. This strategy helped most of the time in the early stages. It did backfire at least one time and Amir had to adjust and try to be careful of what he would tell Nasseem. Once when Amir went to pick him up, he was so excited to go out. Amir knew that he only had about two hours for this whole visit with Uncle Nasseem since he needed to go home on time to pick up his son from the bus stop. He told the nurse that gave him the book to sign him out that they were going to be out for "a little bit, about two hours." Amir must have repeated this more than once that it stuck to Nasseem's mind. After they went out and Amir dropped him back at the center and went home, Amir got a call from Nasseem.

"Hey, Amir, how are you?"

"I am fine, Uncle, how are you?"

"When are you going to come?"

"We were just together uncle, remember, we were out, and I took you back home?"

"Yes, but this was only two hours, I need to spend more time with you; not only two hours."

"Yes, Uncle, but remember I told you I needed to go pick up Michael from the bus stop."

"You only spent two hours with me and that's not enough."

"Okay, Uncle, I will see you next time."

"When are you coming?"

"In few days."

"Okay, bye."

In the beginning, Amir was starting to feel bad that Uncle Nasseem was feeling lonely and wanted to spend some time out of that place. Then he realized that this was not about his visit or the time he spent with him, this was about him proud of himself that he remembered something Amir said. Amir had told the nurse when he was signing him out that they will be out for just about two hours. Nasseem clunk onto these words and remembered them and then used them for a conversation.

"When are you going to come again?" became the question that Nasseem continued to ask over and over. In the beginning, the room that he was in had a phone and he had written down Amir's cell number on a piece of paper. It was okay that he called from time to time with this same question. It, at least, made Amir know that he was okay. The staff in the nursing home were not that keen on the social aspect of his illness. Amir gradually realized that they just wanted to have the correct documentation of what they were obligated to do. Other than that, there was no interaction with him. Amir received calls to "let him know" that he had fell down, but he was okay. When Nasseem started to have behavioral issues, he received many calls to document what was happening.

After some time, Amir believed that although Nasseem was repeatedly asking him about the time that he will be back, Amir's answer was not that important since it was not processed in his mind normally. Nasseem had a calendar in his room so Amir felt it may be helpful to write on the Calendar when he will see him next. He wrote down 'Amir will come' on some days that he thought he will be able to go. It did not matter if he kept the promise since he knew that Nasseem's days were mixed up in his mind. Regardless, Amir kept trying to keep him aware of the months and days as much as he could, but this was only him, Amir, trying to do so. There was no interest from the staff to engage him in realizing even what time of the day it was. Amir's efforts were not making much of a difference. He always wondered if his memory and awareness would have been preserved for a longer time, had he lived with someone like a wife or a family caregiver.

They continued to have their trips outside the center together. It did not feel as a big burden on Amir although he had other things to do but he still felt that he was doing something good. In the past, one thing that he was not able to do for his family was to take care of his father and mother when they were sick before they died. Amir even once told this to Debbie when she was telling him on the phone that whatever he was doing for Nasseem was a "good thing." He told her, "I was not there for my father when my mother was taking care of him when he had dementia, to me I feel that at least I get to do something." Amir was also not there to help his uncle who was taking care of his mother until she passed. Amir also always remembered that his mother used to tell him to take care of Nasseem as if she knew what will happen to him. His response to her was always that "he is older than me and he can take care of himself, I have lots of responsibilities." He was starting to understand what she really meant.

In his effort to try to help Nasseem be aware of things, he continued to try to tell him about what's happening in the world or what season they were in. He got a notebook and every time he went to him, he used to write down what they did. In Amir's mind he felt that if Nasseem happened to open the notebook at any time he will see something like, *10/20/2014, Amir came, went to ShopRite, had haircut.* He was hoping that this will make Nasseem feel that Amir was just there, and they did something together. Their trips continued for a while and although the days did not mean much to Nasseem, Amir was still at this stage interested in trying to engage him in what was happening around him.

When Christmas was approaching Amir thought that if he saw around him some decorations he will be reminded of Christmas. When they went out, he asked him if he would like to get something like a small gift to any of the people that took care of him in the center. This time, instead of not giving any response, he kind of agreed and when they went to the Christmas Tree Shop, Amir helped him pick up three small gifts and got three gift bags to put them in. God knows who these gifts went to and how he gave them to them since Amir did not find them in his closet the next time he visited him and, when he asked if he gave them to anyone there was no response.

Since the Thanksgiving dinner at Amir's house was kind of overwhelming to Nasseem, Amir decided that the next time he invited him, they could be just by themselves.

Christmas time in Amir's family gets to be a little confusing because of the different traditions. The Coptic Orthodox Christmas is celebrated on January 7, about two weeks from the other "normal" Christmas. Growing up in Egypt in the 1970s and '80s, the way Amir celebrated Christmas was very simple and different. On Christmas Eve, they would either go to church for a midnight mass or stay home to have dinner after midnight. In the Coptic Church's traditions, there are many scheduled fastings that most people try to follow, especially if you are living in Egypt. The period of "fasting" before Christmas is forty-three days. This is based on the Bible's mentioning of the forty years the Israelites spent in the desert and the Egyptians added three days after a miracle that occurred in the tenth century A.D. in Cairo, Egypt. (When a mountain near Cairo was said to have moved with the prayers of the congregation). The fasting in the Coptic Church is observed by abstaining from any food that comes from any animal. In other words, the "Copts" (as they are usually called) become vegan for that time except for fish, which is allowed on certain days. This was also the same for the lent period but for lent, fish is not allowed for the whole fifty-five days of lent. As much as Amir and his family considered themselves a religious family, they didn't fast the whole period and they mostly ended up fasting about the last four weeks for the pre-Christmas fast and about five weeks of the lent.

As a child, on Christmas eve, Amir would be waiting until the clock tick at midnight, that's when he could break the fast. And this meant that after days of eating vegetables, beans and some fish, they could have meat, chicken, eggs and, most importantly, chocolate and ice-cream. On Christmas day, he would go to the Church's Christmas party in the morning then he came home and had dinner with his family. The only gift him and his sister would get was money that his parents gave them besides the fact that they got them new clothes.

This kind of traditions were not going to work well for Amir's kids in the United States in which Christmas is so commercialized and all the kids, even non-Christians, expect gifts. Amir and his wife had to go along with this and for their kids they would get them Christmas gifts and give it to them on December 25. The kids knew that 'Santa' was not going to make a special visit for them and he had to come on the same day for all the kids. He also, however, on some years had to show up at a different time during the day if it happened that dad had to spend Christmas eve at the hospital and was not home until later in the day on Christmas. Dad would have to come first then, suddenly, Santa's gifts arrive after him. During the Christmas time, the family continued with their fast and could not eat the cookies, pies, eggnogs etc. that people ate during that time and around the New Year. When January 7 came, they broke their fast in their traditional way and celebrated in a more religious way, with no gifts. Most families in their church have resorted to this compromise with some differences from one family to the other. They recently learned that even back home in Egypt, Christmas is starting to be as commercialized. It appears that businesses and merchants in Egypt caught up on the benefits of advertising and promoting products during that time of the year.

Amir planned to have Nasseem come on the day after Christmas, which meant the day after the kids and everyone opened their gifts. To his surprise, he got a call from him on the 25th, just to say, "Merry Christmas!" Amir could sense a pride in Nasseem's voice that he remembered what day it was. He was certain that somebody must have told him that it was Christmas, but to make the connection that it was a good time to call Amir and wish him a Merry Christmas was very impressive and confusing to Amir. It was at a time when Nasseem did not make many connections with other simpler things.

Why did he remember certain things? He made Amir worry many times that he didn't belong in that rehab center. Other times, Amir thanked God that Nasseem was there. It was expected that Nasseem remembered the old stuff since short term memory loss is the one affected. When they would be getting ready to go out, he would not give him an answer whether he already had lunch or dinner. One-time Amir asked the aide in front of Nasseem whether he had eaten or not and the aide turned to Nasseem and told him to answer. Of course Nassem did not say anything. Amir sometimes felt that Nasseem did not want to lose an opportunity to taste some outside food that was different from the nursing home food. He didn't blame him, but he needed to know sometimes whether they were keeping track of his nutrition or not.

When Amir invited Nasseem to come for a Christmas dinner, he told him that it was going to be just fish. When they were going in the hallway, he noticed some of aides that used to help him. He made sure to stop to make them notice that he was going out for dinner at his nephew's house. Amir was shocked to see him even give a hug and a kiss to one of the aides. Nasseem never liked touching. In fact, he had gotten into trouble by not liking to touch people. He had once worked as a patient transporter in a hospital while he was working on his master's degree. As far as Amir remembered, one time while he was transporting a patient on a stretcher, he dropped the old lady on the floor. This was not what got him in trouble. The fact that he did not want to touch her to help her get up was the problem and she ended up suing the hospital. This time he kissed and hugged a person that he had no connection with. Although Amir was surprised, he was pleased to see him becoming more comfortable in the center. On this visit to Amir's house Nasseem did also fine interacting with Amir's family. He took him back to the center not knowing at that time that although there were still other Christmases in Nasseem's life, this was the last time for him to visit and see Amir's family.

After few of their trips together, Amir slowly learned that he had to stop asking Nasseem questions at times when he was doing something else. If they were walking trying to get to the car or walking in an aisle of the supermarket and suddenly Amir decided to ask a question like, "Where do you want to go first?"

"Do you want to get some crackers?"

Nasseem's immediate reaction was to stop the current action, i.e., walking, followed by silence and lips movement with no answer at all. Amir would then realize that he made a mistake of asking the question since Nasseem could not move anymore because he was trying to think, and he will not come up with an answer anyways. He remembered what Debbie had told him before she went to Mexico, that when she took him out for his haircut and some food shopping, she wanted to treat him to a meal, so she took him to Panera Bread. She said that after they sat down, the menu was so confusing to him and she had to help him choose. This was even long before he had gotten much worse during the times that Amir was taking him out.

Amir gradually learned to offer the answers to his own questions and try to make Nasseem feel that there were no more questions so they can go on and continue walking. In the very beginning, Nasseem was able to articulate some of the things he liked, and Amir took note of them so that when they went out the following times, he would go to an aisle that he knew Nasseem would like something in. He would then stop and pick it up from the shelf. Nasseem would now then say "yeh" as in approving what Amir was choosing. This worked for Iced-tea, Coke and food items that Amir knew he liked and needed. The problem was that as soon as he would get to the men's care aisle he always asked to get aftershave and razors when Amir knew that he had plenty of them in his room and he did not need anymore. Amir always thought that, one day he, himself will have Nasseem's same problem and he wondered which aisle will he be stopping at repeatedly to get something? He had a feeling that no matter where his brain function was going, he will always be interested in getting a cake or cookies. He hoped that when that time comes someone will be with him helping him just like what he was doing with Nasseem.

At times, Amir wanted to give uncle Nasseem some freedom from him for at least few seconds so he would feel that he was free. While they were shopping, Amir would intentionally leave him by himself as soon as he realizes that Nasseem noticed something and getting interested in looking at. Amir would keep his eyes on him and walk away to let him enjoy his moment by himself. Most of the times he would just continue to keep looking at whatever he was looking at until Amir came back.

In the beginning, he once did something that he further regretted. Amir once left him in the car until he went inside Chick-fil-A to order and get him a sandwich. It was night time and Amir felt that Nasseem will not dare to come out of the car especially that Amir had the keys and locked the car. Nothing happened, but he kept worrying while he was waiting in line for the order. He then realized that it was not a good idea to do so. One time they went to the Christmas Tree shop and it was the Holiday time when every place was crowded. Coming out of the store, Amir felt that it will take forever for him to walk, in the freezing cold, to where they parked the car, so he asked him to just stand there and wait for him. Amir ran to the car while wondering that Nasseem might start realizing that he should be looking for him. Luckily in those two times, everything was okay.

When Amir would drop him off at the center and if they had shopping bags, he sometimes would let him get out of the car and take him to the door and waited until he went through the door. Then he would tell him to wait for him until he parked the car and brought the shopping. In the beginning, he was able to find his way to the room but as his memory got worse, he would stay in the hallway until Amir came back or until someone found him and took him to the room. He had a bracelet that was on his wrist all the times and it would alarm when he got close to an exit door.

Most of the times when they were out nobody noticed that something was wrong with him. It just seemed like Amir is out with his elderly father. Amir somewhat liked this feeling, to fulfill the feeling that he never helped his father during the time that he needed him. Nasseem's knee problem made it appear more like he was just having trouble walking as expected from an elderly person. If Amir said "sorry" to someone who was trying to be nice and hold the door for them because it was taking him long time to move, they would say "that's fine we all will be slow at some point."

The only time that it was noticeable that he had dementia was when they went to a small family restaurant and the waitress brought them the menu. Amir knew what he was getting since it was before Christmas and he could only eat French fries, but he was trying to help Nasseem make a choice. It was not easy to try to tell him what to get, something that he could easily tell his seven-year-old son to do, and at the same time, try to avoid all the stress that he was having trying to make sense of the menu. When they finally finished eating and he went to the restroom, the waitress came to Amir and said, "Does your father have dementia?"

In his mind Amir thought, *"Yes! she felt that he was my father, I must be doing something right."*

"Yes, my uncle has dementia," he answered.

Amir started to feel that when he took him out to try to shop for food and then went to get a bite somewhere it took so long. He decided that it would be easier to just go to the supermarket on his way to the center and pick up what he needed, then go to him and if everything was okay, he could then take him out. He had learned what his uncle liked, and it was easier for him to just stop by – quickly pick up the Mortadella, Swiss Cheese, Deli style shrimp salad…etc. That worked because his interest in having a haircut was more than any kind of shopping. They would then go out for his haircut and get a bite at a fast-food place then he would take him back.

Nasseem had been in the center for more than three months already and Amir was starting to feel comfortable that he was getting used to the place. At least he was not resisting going back when they went out together. Nevertheless, Amir was still receiving calls from him asking about when he would come. One time he asked,

"When are you coming to take me home?"

"Uncle Nasseem, where do you want to go?

"165 Shobra Street, Cairo."

For a long time, Amir's answer remained the same; that they owed a lot of money to the center and they had to wait until the insurance paid the money. Most of the times he accepted this answer. Sure, when Amir would visit after a phone conversation like this, he was concerned that this idea of going home will come back. Luckily, it seemed that his interest in going out at that time took over and he would be happy to be going out shopping and did not mention anything about going home.

Chapter Nine
To Care or Not to Care?

By nature, Amir had a tendency to not complain much. Only when something really bothered him. Once during a meeting in his division, he felt that he had to say something in disagreement with what his director had said to defend himself. Since he believed he was right he did not hide that. It was the first time for his director to see him obviously upset. The next day he ran into the director in the hallway and the subject came up. Amir said, "I'm sorry if I seemed upset in the meeting." His director told him that he was shocked but, in a way, glad to know that if something concerned him, he would let him know.

Amir also described himself as a chronic worrier and since he was so worried about the Medicaid approval that was probably why he ignored so many things that were bothering him with the care that Nasseem was getting in the center. Having worked in the medical field, he knew that a big factor in the care that you get as a patient is the person who is delivering that care. Sure, there is the effect of the system itself, but personalities play a huge factor. Amir knew that Uncle Naseem favored some of his caregivers more than others and in turn, some of them did not treat him as well, as they got the feeling that he didn't like them.

There was still no justification for some of the things that were going on.

The simplest thing was the laundry. Amir had brought to the center many pairs of underwear and lots of clothes (some of them he bought new and some he got from Nasseem's apartment). Amir thought that he should have enough clothes when they took the laundry until it came back. It was strange how this was handled. One thing that he would have expected that someone would be keeping track of where his dirty clothes were and put them in a hamper for further collection. This was never the case and it appeared to Amir that their expectation was that Nasseem will put his dirty clothes in the hamper for them to take.

How did people who care for people with dementia all the time had this expectation from someone who is so confused about everything? What made it worse was that Amir was not there frequently enough to help him. The mesh hamper bag that they had in the room for him to fill would have one or two pairs of underwear, the other hamper that supposed to have the clean clothes would have one dirty underwear and one clean. Amir thought that it was a simple task that whoever brought in the clean clothes would just have emptied it and put them in his closet. This was never the case. Nasseem had a trash can in his room that he used to put in both the trash and his clothes. As things progressed with his confusion and limited mobility, there were so many times that his dirty clothes ended up in the trash basket. They would be left there for weeks. At first, Amir thought that if he drew the nurse's attention to this and asked her to have someone pick up his laundry, that's good enough. He subsequently learned that that was not good enough and he had to separate the clothes from the trash and place the clothes in the mesh hamper bag that was in the room. Amir had to bring the bag outside to the nurse and ask her where she wanted him to put it.

Week after week, his closet was having less and less clothes that he could use, and some clothes were not even his. It was not a big surprise to Amir to see that Nasseem was not getting a good care at that facility. He had heard many times on the news about nursing homes abuse and neglect and he knew that this was something that, without a doubt, existed. There was, however, a difference between being elderly with multiple illnesses than having dementia in addition. When Uncle Nasseem came to the center, he almost had no physical problems. His dementia was his main problem and it became obvious that there was nothing that this center would offer to make it better or to help him through it. Amir didn't know if there was any other available centers that could have taken better care of him. He did not try to find out because he knew that the cost was going to be a big problem. Not only this, Nasseem started to exhibit behavioral problems that made Amir feel that nothing is going to work, and he just had to give them a chance.

Nasseem was not cooperating with the caregivers and Amir got complaints that he would not let certain people help him with bathing. He was not letting them clean the room when they wanted. It usually happened when he would just be getting up late in the morning. Amir knew that his sleep cycle was not working well. Even before he got problems, he used to stay up late and wake up very late, but then he was living by himself with no rules that he needed to follow. He was also in general not a rule follower, wanting to do what he wanted to do which was one of the reasons he had employment and relationship issues. This was not working well for the caregivers in the center. Some of the caregivers tried to accommodate his needs by leaving his care for the last on their assignment so he will be up and some just gave up on giving him care altogether. They would just go into his room from time to time to make sure that he was still alive. He would still greet many of them who walked in his room by saying "get out." He sometimes shouted that in English and sometimes in Arabic, which they did not understand but got the idea that they were not welcomed in his room.

At the rehab center, they were starting to have renovations in some of the rooms and they were going from one hallway to another. On one of Amir's visits, the nurse came to tell him that the hallway that he was in was going to be next in line for the renovations and he will be moved to another room. Amir felt that he had just gotten comfortable with the location of his room and was able to find the dining hall that he had his lunch in from time to time. He wasn't sure how Nasseem was going to handle the move and whether it will make him get confused. There was no choice. The nurse told him that they should be able to bring him back to his room within a month or so.

For the next few times Amir visited him, he tried to tell him that they will be moving him to another room. He also wrote that in the notebook that he had in his room. Few days later Amir got a call from the nursing supervisor telling him that he was moved and gave him the new room number.

Continuing along with their tradition in the center, they ignored the fact that he did not have the mental capacity to be able to fix the place that he was in. When Amir visited him in the new room, he found that they were, surprisingly, good in packing everything for him but that was just it. All his belongings were in plastic bags on the floor in the room. Amir started unpacking and he soon found out that it was going to take more than one visit to have things back in order. That also meant that he was not going to be able to take him out on his visits since he will have to use some of the time that he puts aside for the visit in cleaning and organizing the room. The new room itself was renovated and the bathroom was also renovated. Amir had to emphasize to him that the room was nice, and he was surprised that Nasseem's response was, "Go check out the bathroom!" Amir then realized that he didn't have to worry about him being more confused since Nasseem seemed to like the new room and was impressed with the new bathroom.

Now Amir had to only worry about cleaning the mess, connecting the VCR again, trying to find a place to put the DVD player, connect the phone…etc. He was getting ready to leave when he noticed that there was no dial tone in the phone when he plugged it into the wall jack. On his way out, he talked to his nurse and told her that the phone was not working, and she said that when they renovated the rooms, something happened to the phone lines and she will let someone know. This issue was never fixed, Uncle Nasseem got a new room but lost the phone forever! This also resulted in Amir not getting any phone calls from Nasseem anymore. It seemed that Nasseem did not care about that. Amir thought that it was one less stressful thing for Nasseem not to be looking for the piece of paper that had Amir's phone number which was also lost in the move.

The new room was at the end of the hallway and next to it was an exit door which alarmed every time someone with a security band got too close to the door. Nasseem was always disturbed from those alarm sounds. He also quit trying to find the dining hall since the new hallway looked different to him. With Nasseem being less mobile his feet started to get swollen and it was very hard for him to wear the dressy shoes that he always liked. Amir could not convince him to use a pair of sneakers that he got for him despite that they fit him well. He never wore sneakers in his life. He always liked to have many pairs of leather dress shoes and he would buy many when he went to Egypt since there you can get real leather shoes for one fourth the price in the US. Every time they would be going out Amir tried to have him wear the sneakers, but he insisted on wearing the tight leather ones. Amir had to give up. They continued to have hardly any conversation in the car or when they sat down to eat in a restaurant.

Amir intentionally played some Arabic songs in the car for his favorite singer "Abdel Haleem." Abdel Haleem was a famous Egyptian singer and Uncle Nasseem used to memorize his songs and would recognize from the music which song it was. In the car when the music started, Amir would ask, "Do you know which song is this?" and sometimes he got the answer right away with the correct song but other times it would be like any other question; Amir only got from him the moving of the lips and the sense that he was struggling with his thoughts and nothing came out of his mouth.

The summer was approaching, and Amir and his wife had decided that it was about time to try to take the kids to see Egypt. His older son had been once to Egypt when he was eighteen months old and the youngest one had never been there. Until Amir's mother passed away three years earlier, he had been going by himself to see her every year or every other year. He would only stay there for one week which when you add the time you spend traveling it adds up to about ten days and he had to be off one day before and at least one day after coming back and that makes about the two weeks' vacation that he was able to get at work at one time. This time Amir was trying to arrange it so they can take the kids to see Egypt as tourists, in other words more sightseeing than "family seeing." Anyway, the only family they needed to see was Amir's sister and the kids' cousins. This time Amir was able to take three weeks off.

They started planning from January and purchased the airline tickets in February to travel in the beginning of July. They knew that it was not the best time to be in Egypt since it was going to be very hot, but they did not have a choice. It was his older son's summer vacation before senior year in high school and they knew that the following year will be hard as he would be preparing for college. They planned and planned and had every day's plans arranged, hotels reserved, and transportation arranged.

Overall, the trip was successful, and both their sons enjoyed it. They saw the Pyramids of Giza, the sphinx, Egyptian Museum in Cairo, some of the ancient Coptic Churches which were built in places that were known to be part of the Holy Family's trip to Egypt. They also went to Luxor and they saw many of the Pharaoh's temples. It was exhausting but they felt that it was something they needed to do for a long time. Surprisingly, also that although his sons had never perfected the Arabic language, they were able to communicate and talk to people in Arabic that sometimes nobody noticed that they actually did not know how to speak it well.

Amir was so worried of what will happen to Nasseem when they were away. He knew he was not going to call him since he did not have the phone anyway, but he was worried that something will happen, and they would not be able to reach him. On the day that they were travelling, he stopped by the supermarket and picked up some items that Nasseem liked and took it to him and put them in the fridge. He stopped by the social worker's office to tell her that he will not be available for a little more than two weeks and he made sure that she had Debbie's phone number. Amir did not have time to stay with him and he used one of his usual excuses that he had to go pick up his son from school.

Amir's prayers were heard that nothing happened while they were away and, luckily, nothing happened also after they came back. Just a day after they were back, Amir got very sick and he started to throw up and could not keep any food down. It was strange since if it were an infection, it would have been something that more than one person in the family would have since they were together all the time. He was glad that they were all well but at the same time, he was confused about what was happening to him.

It was on Amir's first day back at work when he started to have nausea and he was by himself in his office in the hospital. He was there for few hours and he was supposed to leave to go to do rounds with the nurse practitioner in the other hospital that they covered.

He was on the phone talking to one of the physicians in his group when he told her that he didn't feel well, so she asked if she should tell somebody to check on him and he agreed and hung up the phone and started throwing up. In just a few seconds about five people were at his door trying to figure out what was wrong with him. The next thing he remembered was being in the emergency room. He didn't remember how he was taken from his office on the third floor to the ER on the first floor. What he remembered was a strange feeling of letting go. For a moment he felt like this was it, he was going to die, and, in his mind, he thought, *Is this it? Did I need to show the kids where I came from and to say goodbye to my sister?* If that was the case, he had to thank the Lord that He let him stay alive until he completed that.

Afterwards, he was still thankful that he lived through this time of uncertainty of what was happening to him which did not seem to be anything dangerous since all the tests and x-rays did not show anything wrong with him. Nasseem in the meantime remained protected from all the worries that Amir had to go through concerning his health. Amir had planned to visit him as soon as he became well. While Amir was in the hospital recovering, he got a call from the Medicaid office and it was the person who was handling his appeal for the period that they originally denied to cover for Nasseem. It was going to cost $12,000.00 in payment to the center if they continued to deny it. The Medicaid case worker asked Amir for another document that he needed, and he promised that the appeal will be approved. By then it had taken about seven months for that appeal to be approved. At some point, Amir had given up hope and talked to Debbie about it and she was willing to help come up with the money.

It took about a month from the time Amir visited Nasseem before they went to Egypt until he was able to see him again. Just as Amir was starting to regain his strength back, he got a call from the nurse at the center informing him that they found Nasseem in his room on the floor and apparently, he had fallen. The nurse who called him was telling him that he could not tell them what exactly happened and how he fell. Amir was surprised that after being there for almost a year, they still didn't know what to expect from his mental abilities. Of course, he was not going to be able to tell them anything. She told Amir that he was back to his normal and Amir said that he was going to be visiting soon.

When he went to visit him, he was in bed. Amir was feeling bad that he had not been able to visit him for some time and he wanted to take him out for a little bit. He was in his bed covered with a blanket and when he was telling him to get up Amir realized that he was not wearing pants or underwear. Amir looked in his closet and there was only one pair of underwear that was clean. His soiled clothes were as usual in the hamper mixed with some trash. Amir helped him put the underwear and some pants on and gave his nurse his clothes for the Laundry. Since Amir had come with the intention to take him out, he did not bring with him any food and when he realized that he was not interested in going out he decided to leave the center and go get some food for him. He went to the supermarket and got him some of his favorite items and went back to the center and made him a shrimp salad sandwich to have with a bottle of Coke.

Few days later, Amir got a call from the nurse telling him that the doctor that rounded in the center was concerned that Nasseem might have DVT (deep vein thrombosis), she said that he ordered for him to have a Doppler done on his leg to confirm the diagnosis but Nasseem was refusing to go with them to have it done. She said the famous phrase that Amir heard repeatedly, "I just wanted to let you know." This is the phrase that usually preceded the note that she had to put in the chart indicating that the family was notified. Amir answered her that they should try to convince him to have it done and thanked her. A day later she called him and told him that they were able to have the Doppler done and they confirmed the DVT diagnosis and the doctor prescribed some medicine, but he does not want to take it.

The next day a nurse called Amir to tell him that they had to send him to the hospital since he did not want to take the medicine. Amir knew that this was not going to go well with him. If he was already refusing the medication in the center where he was, at least, becoming familiar with, how was he going to react in a new place with new faces that all they needed from him was to poke him with needles and IV's. When Amir was able to get some time off to go visit him, he went to the hospital. He brought with him his favorite Chick-Fil-A sandwich and got him a small fruit tart.

As soon as Amir got off the elevator on the floor where he was and asked about his room, the nurse greeted him with the complaint that he was not allowing her to give him the medication. He had developed fever and they thought that he had an infection along with the DVT. Amir told her that he'll talk to him. He knew that nothing will make sense to him, but he had to try anyway. He went in the room and greeted him and told him about the sandwich then the nurse came and was preparing to hook up the medicine to his IV. He looked at her angrily and said, "No." Amir started explaining about the infection and the DVT and he told him that if he didn't take the medicine he would die.

Amir didn't think that he comprehended anything he said but he ended up taking the medicine anyway. The nurse also told Amir that they had to put him in a special bed since he fell from the regular bed on his first night in the hospital. Amir visited him another time in the hospital and had the same scenario of helping the nurse while she was giving him the medicine. This was not a strategy that Amir necessarily liked; that they waited until he came to visit to be able to give the medicine. It, however, worked for three days. Afterwards Amir got a call from the doctor telling him that Nasseem was stable enough to go back to the center, but he needed to continue heparin subcutaneous injections which they can give in the center.

When he went back to the center, he found that they have moved him to another room that was closer to the nurses' station since he became a "Fall Risk."

The following weeks were challenging to the nurses. Now that they are the ones to give him the injections and it was a real injection not something that they put in an IV, Amir expected it to be even harder. He received calls after calls telling him that he is refusing to allow them to give him the injections. He had become combative and he fought them and kicked them when they got near him. Again, when

Amir visited him at times, he was able to distract him enough for them to give him the injection. He went one time and one of the nurses told him that she cannot take it anymore since he kicked and fought, and another nurse was going to try to give it to him.

Amir was waiting at the nurses' station until they went in to try to give him the injection and as soon as the nurse went in the room Amir heard him shouting so Amir went in. Nasseem had gotten out of bed and was yelling and trying to hit the nurse. Amir was trying to stop him, and he didn't know what to do, he just found himself slapping him on the wrist. The look that Nasseem gave him at that time Amir never forgot. It was like "How dare you do this?" Amir did not stop there, he went on and said, "This is not acceptable, you have to listen to them."

Things continued to get worse with his behavior that Amir got calls almost every day if not twice a day. Sometimes complaining that he refused to take the medicine "just to let you know" and sometimes complaining that he shouted at them in Arabic and they wanted to know what he meant.

The way things were going in November and December of 2014 made Amir wonder for how long this can go on. Uncle Nasseem's deterioration was fast and he was not yet able to get time to read about the nature of his disease. Amir remained unprepared and he didn't know what to expect next and how Nasseem's further deteriorations will be handled. He continued to receive phone calls not only about the injections but also about the pills he was supposed to take. He wondered why they were easily giving up on him. One reason, Amir thought, was that they had seen these situations repeatedly in the center and they must have come to realize that there was no benefit of fighting all the time about giving a treatment to someone who is not aware of the need for it.

If you were in the right state of mind, you would understand that having a complicated DVT will mean that you are at risk of dying at any time if the thrombus migrated to your lungs, your brain or your heart. If you couldn't comprehend this, it did not make sense to accept any treatment that anybody is trying to give you. The calls gradually became that he not only refused but he shouted at them and was yelling with a foreign language (Kelab/Abouky). Amir's response was that they must be more familiar than him in how to deal with this kind of behavior.

He was there one weekend and the nurse approached him and told him that he should start to consider comfort care. This meant that they would try to keep him comfortable. 'Comfort care' was not a new term to Amir, having worked in the NICU. The way they use this term in the NICU might be different, but it basically meant to him DNR (do not resuscitate) which meant that there was no reason to revive him if needed. To make this decision that affects someone's life may sound very hard on some people. Amir's immediate response to her was that he was not ready yet and he would need to discuss it with other family members. Amir, technically, did not have to discuss it with anybody since he was his guardian. He only had to sign a paper and that was about it. Deep down he believed that if Uncle Naseem was not happy and was fighting with the staff and not comprehending what he is fighting about, he will be less miserable if they left him alone.

It took a little while for Amir to convince himself that this was the best thing to do for Nasseem but the part in him that felt that this will also be the best for Amir himself made him hesitant. This matter was not about Amir, it was about Nasseem. It did not take long from Amir to give up his reluctance. After he visited him on the Sunday of the Thanksgiving weekend and saw how he treated the staff and how he was trying to hit the nurse, he believed that Nasseem only needed to be calmer and have few days of peace. Few days later, they called him at night telling him that he became very violent and came to the nurses' station and hit the computer and broke it.

They called the crisis center and he was going there. Few hours later, they called from the crisis center asking Amir if his uncle had dementia. Amir was surprised because he thought that if they had called the crisis center for him wouldn't they have given some report? It turned out that the crisis center didn't deal with people whose main problem was dementia, Amir then realized that the staff of Sunshine Center chose to withhold this information just to be able to send him out of the center at least for some time. At the crisis center, they told him that he was calm after they gave him medications and they cannot keep him and will send him back. The next day the social worker called Amir and told him that she needed to talk to him, and they arranged for a meeting few days later.

Amir met with the social worker and the nurse manager on December 5 and they asked him to sign for comfort care, DNR (do not resuscitate), DNI (do not intubate). This kinds of meetings Amir were so familiar with. In his job of treating newborns in the Neonatal Intensive Care Unit (NICU) many times the treatment team decides that the time is appropriate to discuss with the baby's family DNR. The emotions in these kinds of meetings are usually high and many times Amir finds himself fighting hard to conceal his tears and emotions from showing in front of the families. In these cases, he usually presents it to the family as "we did everything we could, and we don't have anything else to offer to your baby." It is at this moment that himself and the team question themselves, *Is this the truth? Could they do something more for the baby? Are they hurting the baby and the family more if they are continuing to do what they are doing? Is it really the right time to give up?* These are all questions that the team try to protect the family from noticing them while presenting the honest opinion on the baby's condition.

In many of these meetings Amir would face a family that is not ready to give up and want the team to continue doing what they were doing, and the team had to honor their request despite feeling that it is not necessary. What happens next is that 'nature' takes its course and the baby passes despite all the efforts or the family comes to a realization that they should stop the support.

The case with Uncle Nasseem was different since Amir was already feeling bad that he was continuing to suffer and his attitude toward the treatment is causing him to have one complication after the other. He signed the DNR and DNI papers. He also signed for not to put a gastric tube but to consider hospitalization if needed. It was getting close to the Christmas time and Amir was trying to figure out what he should get Uncle Nasseem for Christmas. He remembered that when he went shopping with his family on Black Friday, he got him a pair of slippers and he had it at home to give it to him. After he signed the papers, he went to his room and gave him the slippers. Sure, he did not even try to mention that they were an "early" Christmas present since this was not going to mean anything to him.

Despite signing the papers Amir still had mixed emotions about it because of his previous experience with other family members. Amir wasn't there when his father's Alzheimer was progressing and worsening. His mother was his caregiver in the sense of taking care of all what the nurses in the nursing home were dealing with, with Uncle Nasseem. So, when his mom told him on the phone that she is not sending his dad to the hospital for tube feeding as suggested by some friends, he supported her decision. His dad did not last long after that and Amir felt that this was a blessing. His dad was even younger than Uncle Naseem when he died, besides, he was "his dad."

Again, when his mother was suffering from complications from knee surgeries and leg infections, Amir wasn't there and when they called him to tell him that she passed, he was relieved that her suffering had ended. Not only her suffering but the suffering of her caregiver, his paternal uncle who passed away just d two weeks after her. His mom was also just at Uncle Nasseem's age at the time she died.

In his book, *Being Mortal*, Atul Gawande, MD, elegantly described how it is sometimes complicated to consider withholding further treatments. Letting the patient have peaceful days before dying in many times is a better choice than continuing treatments that are not necessary. This, however, needs the collaboration of the patient, the family and the treating team.

Altogether, Amir tended to think that the person who is suffering is better off when the suffering ends. Letting nature take its course and accepting what happens, to Amir was an acceptable and better alternative. Amir's mixed emotions came from the fact that if he tended to be less aggressive with those who were closer to him than Nasseem, couldn't he do the same in the case of Uncle Nasseem. The flip side was that he was not there for his mom or his dad and he wondered that since he was there for Uncle Naseem if he should do something different.

Amir also knew from his experience with changing the code status is that many times as soon as it is changed in the records, nothing happens to the individual and nothing threatens his/her survival for a while. Therefore, he knew that the journey with Uncle Nasseem was not going to be over soon and he was not sure if it was affecting him mentally or his mind was totally distancing it from him and letting him deal with everything else in his life as if nothing was happening. Many times, he went to him and found him in his bed trying to put on his underwear. It was apparent that he had an accident and was trying to change. All being unnoticed by the staff.

Amir couldn't take him out for a while after he went back to the center from the hospital. He was worried that he will become violent, although he had never been violent toward him. He did not want to risk trying to bring him to his house for dinner like what they did a year ago. He wasn't sure of how he was going to behave in front of his kids, his wife and her family. Besides, the year before he was able to call and tell the staff to tell him to get dressed and be prepared for him when he came. Now, he didn't seem to comprehend any of the things anyone told him.

When they were able to go out again, it was a bit easier for Amir to take him in his wheel chair to his favorite place (haircut). Taking care of his hair used to be one of his passions and for some reason he had never lost this passion. He took him to get a haircut on December 23. That turned out to be a bad idea since the place was packed, and the wait was for 50 min. This was also the first time he took him out after he became violent sometimes in the center and Amir was still quite worried that he would exhibit some strange behavior in front of the people in the store. When they were waiting for his turn, Nasseem turned to Amir and said,

"Can we change?"

"Change what?"

"The color."

"You mean your hair color?

"Yes."

"They don't do this here."

"Okay."

This conversation ended safely. Then the next thing was when Amir was trying to tell the lady cutting his hair to use the clippers instead of the scissors, he interrupted him saying to her, "You don't talk to him, it's my hair not his hair." Amir stopped there, he didn't want him to start to get upset and then who knows what the extent of it would be. It was later that Amir found out that this was the last time that they were able to go out together.

Nasseem's left leg got progressively swollen and it was winter time with one snow storm after the other so it was making sense to Amir that he should not risk him slipping on the snow if they tried going out together. The last time they went out it was very hard for him to get in the car. Other than the size of his leg, he was having difficulty bending and moving his leg. It was so difficult to get into Amir's, Honda Pilot, SUV. He did not think too much about that since his mother-in-law who is older than Nasseem and had knee problems, always had difficulty getting in his car. That time it took him a while to get Nasseem in the car but he had to be in the back seat. This all started to make sense later when he learned in March that they found out that he had a hip fracture which they thought was an old one.

As much as the winter was snowy and stormy, having the DNR status for Nasseem made the nurses and the care givers much calmer and happier. They no longer needed to fight with him about medicine and he was welcoming their visit in his room because it almost only happened when they were bringing in his meals.

Having watched Nasseem's reaction to meals opened Amir's eyes to how we "humans" have these natural desires that are part of us, and we don't necessarily need a fully functioning brain to preserve it. Many times, when Amir brought Nasseem something to eat that he knew he liked he would be excited, (in his own way) he would start eating quickly as if he was worried that someone will take it from him. It seemed to Amir that this was our instinct, trying to keep our body alive. When Amir had stomach and digestive problems, he had days that he had to push himself to eat but he had no appetite. When it turned out that there was nothing wrong with him, he was and still wondering why he was not interested in eating. Whether his brain was working too much worrying about feeling sick after eating and worrying about throwing up or he was having a big problem he could not sort that out at that time. Watching Nasseem's reaction to food made him wonder that he should give his brain a break from thinking too much and just try to eat and worry about what happens later. Nasseem enjoying something he liked was nevertheless, a rewarding experience to Amir just like the times when his sons did not give him hard time when he was trying to feed them something when they were little.

Chapter Ten
The Non-Caregiver

Many caregivers of a loved one with dementia wrote their own experience watching someone deteriorate while feeling the burden of taking care of him/her. This experience is without a doubt emotionally draining. In Amir's situation, he was shielded from providing the actual care; it was all left to the staff at the nursing center. It was like when people say that the grandparents get the luxury of interacting and playing with their grandchildren and at the end of the day; they do not have to do the work that the parents must do.

Most of the caregivers at the center taking care of several elderly people, don't interact with their patients. Amir learned that, not every dementia patient exhibited the same symptoms and signs. He was also certain that a person's behavior could be different at the nursing facility from the behavior among people they are more familiar with and interacted with before the mind and memory flew away.

Amir's paternal uncle who lived with them in the same apartment in Egypt as long as Amir remembered, became the caregiver for his mother when she was sick with multiple medical problems. His uncle had called their apartment where his brother, Amir's father, and his family lived, home for most of his adult life. He was an anesthesiologist and he worked in a hospital in Alexandria for a long time then he worked in several Arab countries for several years before he retired and came back to Alexandria. After Amir's father passed away and his mother became sick, his uncle did not have a choice but to take care of his sister-in-law since Amir was in the US and his only sister lived in a different city. That time that he cared for her was by no doubt a stressful time for him but being a physician, he took care of her as a physician besides being a family member.

Amir was only able to visit his mother for one week every year or even every other year and he often felt that he was not helpful when he was physically there the same as he was not helpful when he was away. His presence for those short visits would not even give his uncle any break to try to take care of himself. He was taking his job of taking care of her so seriously that his only break was when he woke up at around five o'clock in the morning, drank his coffee, took his medicine and sat on "his" favorite chair in the living room to watch TV until she wakes up. She used to wake up at eleven and that was when his "shift" started until it ended close to midnight when she went to sleep. He did this for years and Amir's mom's health was getting worse.

When Amir got the call one morning in December 2011, just one week before Christmas, that his mother had passed, he felt that his uncle must have been relieved. Amir knew at that time that he was not going to be able to get to Egypt on time for his mother's funeral. In Egypt, the funerals are usually arranged within hours and there is no such thing as to keep the body few days until people arrive from different cities as is done in the US. Amir still wanted to go because he felt that he should at least be with his sister and his uncle whom he never really thanked for his hard work.

He arrived in Egypt the day after the funeral and was surprised to hear that his uncle also was not able to make it to the funeral. It turned out that after his mother passed his uncle had severe back pain and was not able to move. The rest of the five days that Amir spent in Egypt at that time he was trying to get his uncle to be comfortable on some medications and was trying to find out exactly what was wrong with his back. Amir got busy trying to make time for the people who kept calling to plan on coming to their apartment to offer their condolences to him while he was trying to schedule X-rays and doctor's house calls for his uncle. (In Egypt, still some doctors are making house calls except that it is significantly expensive).

On his last day, Amir was waiting for the Cab driver that was going to take him to the airport. The driver was coming at two o'clock in the morning and Amir kept telling his uncle that he should just say goodbye and go to sleep since he was not feeling well. His uncle refused and wanted to wait until Amir left. Amir learned later that after he left, Uncle Fareed got sicker and was admitted to the hospital and went into a coma. He remained on the breathing machine for about two weeks and then he passed. It turned out that from what it seemed to Amir that God had a purpose for him to stay strong and continue doing the work and when the job ended there was no reason for him to stay and he left.

Amir had thought that his uncle should be relieved and should be starting to take care of his health and live the rest of his life relaxed and yet the heavens had other plans for him. Now, when Amir looked back at the few days that he spent in Egypt, he remembered that everyone who came to see him also saw his uncle and when there was someone that stopped by just to say "hi" to Amir and Uncle Fareed would notice he wanted them to come and wanted to say "hi" to them also. To Amir, looking back, he felt that his uncle was trying to say goodbye to everyone before he left, and Amir was not an exception. Amir was the last one he said goodbye to before he went to the hospital.

One of the emotional stresses a family caregiver could experience is wondering of what he/she wishes for the affected person and for himself or herself. After an exhausting day while caring for the dementia-afflicted family member, the caregiver may hope that this doesn't continue for a long time. The guilt from having thoughts like this could even cause more stress.

In case of a non-caregiver family member like in Amir's situation, he also had the thoughts of how long this will go on. Nothing was physically exhausting to him. He only had to stop by the supermarket on his way to visit. He became programmed to pick up some of the items that Nasseem liked or used to like. Two cans of iced-tea, four cups of Peach yogurt (certainly not strawberry), a container of precut fresh fruits, few small bottles of Coca-Cola, a store roasted chicken, ham, cheese, deli shrimp salad and some bread. He then headed to the center, signed at the front desk and then walked the long hallways wondering what shape his uncle was in.

Many times, he went in the room to find Nasseem on the bed with his underwear and no pants or trying to put on his underwear. This task had become very difficult for Nasseem especially after his leg and feet became so swollen. He obviously had frequent accidents that would not be recognized by the staff since they didn't attempt to check on him often enough. And sometimes when they tried to check on him, he did not let them come in the room or help him. Although, he didn't like people to get very close to him, he did allow Amir to help him in situations like these because he had the motivation to finish this task. He knew that if Amir came, there must be something he brought with him. It could be just the grocery items or if he had time to stop by Burger King or Chick-fil-A, Nasseem would be lucky and have one of his favorite sandwiches.

The excitement when he saw these sandwiches were very rewarding to Amir. Although this was Amir's 'routine' when he visited him, there was no routine or a set schedule for when he had to visit. He just did it when he was able to, so there was no real stress that he had to do it. Amir felt that it made sense to him to call himself a non-caregiver of his uncle better than calling himself the "guardian."

Chapter Eleven
A Broken Hip

The spring and summer of 2015 brought to Amir new worries about what was going to happen next. He knew that there will be an end to Nasseem's suffering although he didn't really know whether Nasseem himself recognized that he was suffering. They called from the center to tell him that he was complaining of his leg and they did an X-Ray. It showed that he had a broken femur and they were going to take him to the hospital and the doctors in the hospital would be calling him. Amir was not surprised that he had a fractured femur since one of the not many things that he remembered from adult medicine was how common fracture femur was in elderly people. What really surprised him was that he was able to communicate this with the staff enough to let them do something. He not only did this; he also did not fight with them about getting an X-ray. Maybe that part was not true because, knowing Nasseem, he must have given them a hard time trying to get the X-ray done. Anyway, they now had a problem and they needed to do something about it.

The next call Amir received was from the orthopedic resident telling him that it seemed like he had had the fracture for a while and now there is basically two options.

The first option was to do nothing which will mean that he will have limited ability to walk and the second option was that they would have to perform surgery, which in his case, was only partial hip replacement so that he could restore some mobility. Option number two sounded a little better to Amir since he thought that Nasseem still needed to try to move around. Amir accepted the surgery option and told them that he will be there at seven o'clock the next morning prior to the surgery.

It was Palm Sunday and Amir skipped going to church with his family but planned on going as soon as Nasseem was out of the surgery and awake. In the Coptic orthodox tradition, most people try to make it to church on Palm Sunday for the obvious reason of being a special day, but they also try to make sure to attend a special service after the mass which is meant to be like a "general funeral." The concept behind this "general funeral" is that Palm Sunday marks the beginning of the Christian Holy week in which people would be focusing on contemplating on the last days and events before the crucifixion of Jesus. During the Holy week, in the Coptic traditions, when somebody dies, there is no formal funeral service. They would bring the casket into the church during one of the traditional Holy Week prayers and the deceased would be there for an hour or so then they take the casket for the burial. People therefore try to attend the so called "general funeral" on Palm Sunday as a 'just in case' situation.

Amir went first to Nasseem's hospital room and found him calm in his bed. A male nurse came in to take his vital signs and Nasseem turned to Amir and said in Arabic, "This doctor is so young."

Amir answered, "Yes." A lab technician came to take blood samples so he started to get worried, but she was very good. While she was getting the blood, he noticed that the TV was on and it was the news and a picture of a man came on the screen, so he said, "Who's this?"

Amir answered, "Donald Trump's son-in-law." He looked at Amir with no expression. Amir followed that by saying, "You know Donald Trump?"

He spoke, "Yes."

Amir said, "People say he will be running for the presidency."

As Amir expected there was also no expressions or comments but at least he was distracted enough to forget about the blood drawing. A physician came in the room and introduced himself as being the anesthesiologist and had the consent form for Amir to sign. He told Amir that the DNR/DNI status will be on hold during the surgery. This meant that if a person whose code status is DNR is going for surgery, that person will be put on breathing machine to help his breathing while under anesthesia which is part of the procedure. In other words, he is going to be on the breathing machine for the procedure not to resuscitate him. He also told Amir that if there were any major complications that require him to be resuscitated, they will not do heroic measures. Amir signed the paper for the anesthesiologist who then turned to Uncle Naseem and said *As-salamu alaykum*, which how the Arabs greet each other.

As-salamu alaykum is one of the very first words one would learn when you start learning the language. Although it is a very popular phrase, most Egyptians consider it to be how Muslims greet each other and Christians in Egypt use different phrases for greeting. One of the things that Amir had learned over the years being in the United States that many Americans cannot differentiate between being an Arab and being Muslim. Many think that it is a one thing and he tried many times to explain to people the difference but for some reason, it's not easy to grasp.

He used to think that recent immigrants are better in recognizing the differences between different origins and religions although many times he found that this was not always true. He had had people of Hispanic origin approaching him speaking in Spanish and looked at him suspiciously when he responded that he didn't understand. He had also had Indians asking him if he were Indian. Many kids in his son's school used to ask him how he was related to "King Tut!"

When the anesthesiologist said to Nasseem, "*As-salamu alaykum*," Amir greeted him back by saying "wa alaykum assalam" and asked him if he knew Arabic and he said that he just knew few words. The nurse came to tell them that they had to take Nasseem to the OR area and started to move his bed and Amir followed them in the hallway to the elevator. In the OR holding area, the surgeon explained the procedure and obtained consent. The anesthesiologist then came with his assistant and they wheeled Nasseem to the room. Amir said to him "Good luck!" and looked at the clock. He realized that it was too late to consider going to the Mass and come back so he decided to wait until the surgery was over. He went to the hospital's cafeteria to get something to eat.

Luckily, the cafeteria was open. Having worked in many hospitals, he had had different experiences with hospital cafeterias. Some hospitals were now cutting back on the cafeteria hours to lower the expenses and in some hospitals that he worked in, the cafeteria was closed on the weekends and he used to have to prepare meals for himself to take with him if he was working a long shift.

The surgery took longer than expected. Amir waited back in the room as they advised him and after about three long hours, watching TV, saying some prayers and just closing his eyes, the nurse came and told him that the surgeon would like him to go back down to the operating room area. Amir went and the surgeon came out and told him that things went fine. He said that he believed that the fracture occurred sometime ago because Nasseem's muscles were very stiff to manipulate in order to keep the hip joint that was partially replaced in place. He said that it was possible that that hip joint will dislocate. The doctor also said that he will need physical therapy when he goes back to his center.

As expected, they discharged him from the hospital as soon as possible and this happened just after Amir's next visit the day following the surgery. After the surgery things did not go well. When Nasseem went back to his center, he forcefully refused physical therapy. He also refused to move altogether. He needed three people to lift him and he refused to get out of bed to sit in the wheelchair to be taken to the physical therapy department. If they succeeded in getting him out of bed, he would resist getting out of the wheel chair when he reached the PT department.

Amir once visited and when he did not find him in his room, a nurse told him that they had just taken him to PT and showed him the way. When he got to the PT department, he found him in his wheelchair and three of the staff next to him begging him to cooperate with them and get off the wheelchair and he refused. Amir joined them thinking that he might have an influence on him, and he was wrong. He was there for at least half an hour trying with them until they finally gave up and Amir wheeled him back to his room.

The phone calls started again with the "just to let you know" statements. After they exhausted the attempts to take him to physical therapy, they wanted to let Amir know that they had to cancel the physical therapy since he was refusing it. His care was getting complicated day after day. He was in bed all the time since he was not able to move, and they were telling Amir in order to take care of him they had to get three people to lift him and help cleaning him. Amir was still wondering for how long he will continue to suffer.

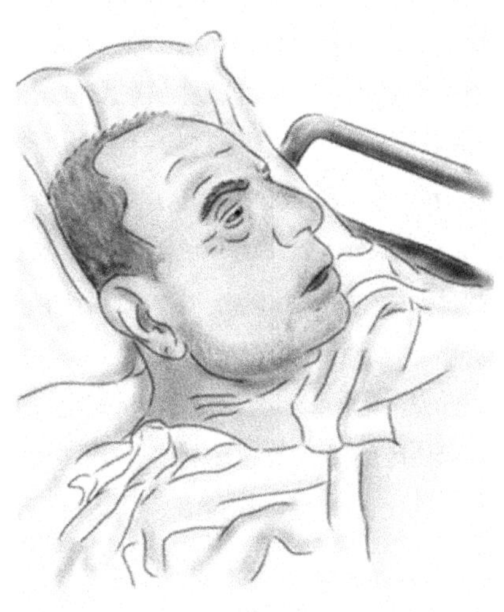

As he was getting busy arranging for his son's high school graduation, Amir received a letter from the center telling him that the center will have a new owner, and they will need to transfer all the residents in the center somewhere else. Amir wasn't that concerned at that time since he was not happy with how his care was being handled. One thing that was still very disturbing was that every time he went, he found his dirty clothes filling the hamper and he had to be the one emptying the hamper and giving them the clothes. It just did not make sense that nobody cared about having his clothes taken to the laundry so that he could have clean clothes that they will be able to put on him. They were complaining that three people needed to lift him and yet they put his clothes in the hamper expecting someone to take it! In a sense, Amir welcomed the news and he knew that Nasseem is in a situation that he will not argue or be difficult since he was not able to move at all and waited for people to give him care. Gina from the center told Amir that they will make contacts with a center that was closer to his house which was even better for him and they were going to take care of all the arrangements; the insurance and the transport.

How do people prepare for their death or the death of someone under their care? Amir had no previous experience concerning what to do regarding this matter. When he started arranging the care for his uncle, it seemed that there was no immediate rush since there was nothing seriously happening to Nasseem especially that he had been surviving one problem after the other. Now that Nasseem's condition was worse, Amir wanted to have some idea of what he needed to do for him in terms of burial arrangements. Still Debbie's words were resonating in his ears, "Nasseem is going to outlive us all since he has more than one doctor for every organ." He started by asking someone in the church who gave him the phone number for Devin who was a "sales person" in a nearby cemetery.

Amir made an appointment and met with Devin who took him around and showed him the crypts and Amir felt that it looked reasonable. He had no idea how much that would cost and when Devin said that it was about $5,000.00, he told him that he would get back to him. After he looked up online the costs of crypts and saw that the range was very wide, he felt that the price that Devin gave him was reasonable. When Devin called him, few days later, asking him if he decided and told him that he can pay it over one year with no interest, Amir felt that was going to be a good deal. The catch was that if they needed to use it any time during that year, they had to pay it off at the time they needed it.

He went back and met with Devin and signed the papers. This was in April and he started his monthly payments a month later. He also contacted the funeral home that the church worked with and asked them if there was anything, he should do in advance considering that he had no idea how soon he will need their services. It turned out that this was not a bad idea. He met with the owner of that funeral home and gave him Uncle Nasseem's info. He then learned that Medicaid pays for a portion of the final expenses and the funeral home submits the papers to Medicaid at the time of the funeral. After meeting with the funeral home owner, he decided that it was not also a bad idea to go ahead and buy him some final clothes and have them ready for him.

When the Sunshine Center was ready to transfer Nasseem they contacted Amir and told him the name of the new center 'Care & More' in Berlin, NJ. They did not need him to be there at the time of transfer, but they asked him to stop by later to pick up the items that will be left behind. When he arrived at the new center, Amir went and met with the administrator to sign some papers and to make sure that the new center will have the social security and pension payment come directly to them instead of the previous center.

The next day he went and got Nasseem's belongings from the Sunshine Rehab center. There were so many things that they did not pack with him when he left including the dirty clothes in the hamper. Amir had to make several trips from the room to the car and on his last trip to the car as he was walking in the hallway, he heard someone calling his name. It was Gina, that was working in the business office and had been helpful throughout the whole process. She said, "I just wanted to say goodbye and wish you and your uncle all the best." She gave him a hug and he thanked her for all her help and left.

That afternoon, Amir spent three hours at the local laundromat washing all the clothes and he got rid of many. He also cleaned the small fridge in his driveway which he soon realized that in Nasseem's new place, there was no room to put it so he kept it in his basement.

Chapter Twelve
Beyond the Second Year, Hospice

It had been two years now since the day Nasseem arrived in NJ and so many things had happened in those two years. When he arrived, he was physically fit and in two years, he became immobile. In the Care & More center, he was being Hoyer lifted for care, to put him in a wheel chair then to put him back in bed. When Amir visited him, he noticed a big change in his attitude. He wasn't showing interest in looking at him or saying anything. Amir started to lose the motivation to go and was dragging himself to do so because he didn't know what to do when he visited. It was hard to believe that it was just the previous December, that he was able to take him to have a haircut and he interrupted him when he was explaining to the stylist what to do and said, "It's my hair not your hair." Nasseem now only associated Amir with drinking Coke since he always brought it with him and helped him drink it. He also seemed to like the few spoons of ice-cream that Amir was feeding him when he visited.

Nasseem would also notice and points to the brown bag or the shopping bag to see if there was something else to eat that Amir brought. Is it ice-cream or just a piece of cake? Somethings were more exciting than others. When Coke and dessert were gone, it was not hard for Amir to say that he was leaving and in response to that there was no reaction from Nasseem.

Until Feb 2016, the only plans were DNR. Amir had signed the DNR papers again when he went to the Care & More center and things remained the same in terms of no real aggressive treatments. The benefit of the new facility was that they had the Hoyer lift, which Amir was not familiar with and had to google and look up some YouTube videos about it. The other place did not have it and his care was restricted to the bed since he had refused altogether anything. With the Hoyer lift they were putting him in a wheelchair with no effort from him and they would wheel him down to the dining hall for a little bit of a change.

Amir got a call from the nursing supervisor and coordinator of care one day in February and she told him that when they discussed his case, they felt that he was eligible for hospice. She told him that they had two hospice companies that they worked with and she would contact one of them. Since Amir did not prefer one company over the other, he told her to call the company of her choice.

Although Amir was usually regarded as a sensitive person that tries to help and think of others before himself, when it came to his reaction to death, it usually seemed to be out of his character. He had experienced death very early on in his childhood. His oldest sister was stricken with cancer when she was thirteen years old. He was seven and at that time in the 1970s, the diagnosis of "cancer" meant pain and eventually death. Although he believed that her specific kind of cancer was still one of the ones that are still hard to treat nowadays, he was sure that the treatment and management would have been different now from that time. She suffered for about ten months and his family also suffered.

When he tries to recall his emotions toward his sister's condition at that time, he feels that everything was mixed up in his brain. He did not know if seeing her going through several operations, hospitalizations and being in pain at home while he did not understand exactly what was going on was a trigger for his sadness. Sometimes he questioned himself that whether what his sister was going through was making him sad or he was sad for the loss of attention that he used to get as the youngest in the family. There was sadness all around, his mother, his dad and his other sister who was the middle child and it seemed that there was no cure for whatever his sister had. At the end, he recalled her being home in bed most of the time in pain taking some expensive medication that his mother's brother, Uncle Ibrahim, had sent from America.

As it is common in Egyptian cities, they lived in an apartment that did not have many rooms to allow everyone to have a room by him/herself. He recalled that his grandmother was visiting to help his mom and he was sleeping in the same room that his sister was sleeping in and he was awakened by his other sister crying. He was half-awake when he asked her why she was crying, and he remembered her saying that their sister was "very, very sick." He did not have any recollection of what happened after this other than everyone was crying and his sister and him being taken away from the apartment to some friends in another apartment building across the street. That family was known to them and they had two girls, one just a year younger than his sister and another girl a year younger than Amir.

Only at that moment, Amir realized that his sister had died. They were all sitting in this friends' apartment and were all crying. He was crying but he also felt that he had to cry even though he was starting to feel that something not that bad happened. His sister was no longer suffering. She was no longer in pain, and that's a great thing. He also realized that they had lost her and that was not a good thing. They were not allowed to go to her funeral, they stayed with their neighbors for few days, only took one day off from school and went back home and tried to go back to their normal routine.

After his sister's death, Amir's both grandmothers died, and he experienced some sadness which he felt was in a more mature 'experienced' way. The sorrow that you go through knowing that things like this happen and life goes on. With more people dying at different ages and different circumstances, it seemed that he developed a sense of control over his reaction to death. He became able to control the extent of grief that he underwent after the passing of any person. Many years later, his dad died after suffering from Alzheimer's and he was thousands of miles away during his fellowship training in Neonatology in the United States. It was not possible for him to go home. He was by himself in his apartment, grieving and yet also feeling the relief that his father's sufferings were gone. Seventeen years later, his mother passed, and he was able to travel and share the mourning with his sister.

The representative from the Hospice called him, he needed to set up an appointment, so they could meet at the center and discuss the care and sign the papers. The meeting was on a Monday at ten o'clock since he was off that day. There was a snow storm over the weekend and his driveway was full of snow. He went out with his wife on that Sunday afternoon while it was still snowing and cleaned the driveway. They expected the school to be closed and he didn't have to work on Monday, but he wanted to keep the appointment with the Hospice people, otherwise he would have had to reschedule. He woke up early on Monday and started to clean the driveway, then he realized that even if he was able to make it, he didn't know if the Hospice person would be. He called Joe, who had contacted him earlier in the week and asked him if they will be able to make it and he told him that the roads by them were clear so they should make it on time.

It turned out that with Hospice, there is some spiritual support and there was a pastor that was in the meeting with Amir and he told Amir that he was familiar with the Coptic Church that Amir went to. They talked about the care that they were going to provide to Naseem in addition to the care in the center.

Chapter Thirteen
A Journey Coming to an End

Amir woke up on August 5, 2016, with Uncle Nasseem on his mind. This was not unusual since he was on his mind most of the time. The thought that he was not doing enough for him always haunted him and he was continuously feeling guilty. There were many things that easily made him feel guilty. The fact that Nasseem was not in a bad shape, health wise, other than the dementia, before he went to the nursing home made it hard on Amir to feel that he did enough to help him. Other than his dementia, he was relatively healthy. That did not mean that Nasseem had viewed himself as healthy. Uncle Nasseem always had some health issue to complain about. In fact, Debbie used to joke many times with Amir and his mom, when she was alive, and she would say, "If you ask Nasseem anytime how he is doing, his answer is: Better." That's because there was always something that he had complained about before.

Amir was always worried that he was not being aggressive enough in investigating and complaining about the care that he was receiving in the nursing home.

It was not hard to notice that he was not receiving the best care at the first nursing home and Amir did not have a choice in the beginning when he did not have his Medicaid, and when he had the Medicaid, he had started to have the behavioral problems and he resisted the treatment for DVT then they tried to avoid him as much as they could and then when he broke his hip his health started to deteriorate.

That morning, like other times, Amir reminded himself that part of Uncle Nasseem's deterioration was his refusal of the treatment and that was one reason that he should not feel guilty about. He planned to visit him within a day or so, especially that he was going away for five days on vacation and knew that he will not be able to have telephone connection for that time so if they called him for any reason, he would not be able to respond.

He was working in his office doing some computer work. He did not have clinical responsibilities. He only had to work in the office, and he had a meeting in the afternoon. While he was in his small office catching up on some e-mails, his cell phone rang, and it was the Rehab Center. When he saw the name on the Caller-ID, his feeling of guilt came back. In his mind he said, "See, I should have visited." The voice of the person on the line was shaky and he could not hear her well, but he knew that the first thing they will ask if it was him and whoever was calling will introduce him/herself. She started with the usual, "I just wanted to let you know," but then her voice changed and continued, "We went to check on Mr. Aziz and we found that he passed."

Amir was not sure if he heard her correctly or not so he asked her to repeat what she had just said. She repeated, "AJ, the nurse had checked on Mr. Aziz earlier and he was in his normal state but when he went back to check on him about two hours later, he found him blue and not breathing, and he…, he passed."

"Oh, my God!" was Amir's response. He wasn't sure what to feel. He was sad, guilty again and again and yet he had this feeling that it's finally over. The lying there with no connection to anything around him is over. She asked if he had pre-arranged anything with a funeral home and Amir gave her the name of the funeral home. Then he asked her if he could go and see him first and she said that it was possible. He told her that he was going to contact the funeral home and get back to her.

Amir hung up the phone and felt lost in his thoughts. He got off his chair and got out of his small office to the hallway. He was in deep thoughts. "What should I do?" His friend Jody, who was just getting out of the elevator and coming in the hallway saw him and felt that there was something wrong. "Is everything okay?" Jody asked him. He told Jody what had happened, that he just got this call and he was not sure what to do. It took him a few minutes until he regained his composure and then he called Hoda and told her. After that, he called the funeral home and told them not to pick up the body until he was able to visit him. He called Debbie and her reaction was almost the same as his. She said, "Thank God!" In the sense that the sufferings had ended. She told him that she had been sick and just had surgery and does not think that she will make it to the funeral. Amir told her that he understood and that he'll let her know what the funeral plans were anyway.

Before he left work, Amir called the rehab center and told them that he was leaving work and would be there in thirty minutes. He also called one of the church board members to ask him about how to initiate funeral arrangements. He was scheduled to a work 24 hours shift the next day and, in his job, it doesn't work well if you change the schedule unless it's an extreme emergency. If he needed to find somebody to work for him, he would have had to arrange to payback the time and things could get disrupted. He therefore thought that he should keep his schedule the same and work the 24 hours shift on that day which was a Thursday. He would be done on Friday morning and then would have the choice to have the funeral either Friday or Saturday especially that he was off the whole weekend. Sunday was not an option because the church had the normal services on Sunday, which is followed by Sunday school which is not done until two in the afternoon.

On his way to the center, Amir felt that he should bring something to the staff. He felt that they were always under stress from the workload and in their type of job they had to deal with tough situations many times. He stopped on his way and picked up two dozen of soft pretzels and headed to the rehab center.

When he got off the elevator on the third floor where Uncle Nasseem's room was, he saw the nurse at the nurses' station. He told the nurse to let the supervisor know that he was there. The supervisor came and she and the nurse took him to the room and the supervisor told him the same things that she had told him over the phone. She said that they were surprised because there were no warning signs that it was going to happen that day. Amir felt that they sounded defensive when he was not questioning anything they said. He still felt that his suffering ended and that was not a bad thing. He told them that he woke up in the morning thinking about him, so it was not a surprise to hear that something had happened to him. He asked them for few private minutes with Uncle Nasseem. They left the room and Amir spent few minutes saying a prayer and thanking the Lord for ending Uncle Nasseem's suffering.

He left the nursing home, went home, had a quick lunch and sat down with his wife trying to figure out which day they should have the funeral on. After going back and forth between Friday and Saturday, they decided that Saturday would work better. He took the clothes that he had bought for him few months before and went back to work since he had a meeting in the afternoon. After work he dropped off the clothes at the funeral home.

When Father George asked if he will be saying anything in the funeral or not Amir was not sure what to answer him and he told him that he would get back to him. He had been trying to write a poem describing his experience, more so, Uncle Nasseem's experience ever since this happened. He had written some finished and unfinished poems in Arabic when he was a teenager and in his twenties. He always found it easier for him to express his feeling through writing. When he came to the US and started to communicate in English most of the times, it became natural for him to try to express himself in English. He was only successful in finishing two poems about a baby's experience in the NICU. Amir remained always sensitive and nervous on how to show his work and for this reason many of his Arabic poems remained handwritten in a notebook and only seen by some of his close friends back in school and college. He also never had the courage to stand in front of a group of people and recite his poems. There were some occasions that he was asked if he could write something that would be presented in a party or gathering, and he did but he always asked others to present it instead of him while he sat nervously wondering how it will be received by the audience.

When he started to get involved in Nasseem's life and watched him deteriorate, Amir started writing some words, but it was not yet completed. When Father George asked the question, it triggered in him the urge to complete it and finish it and use it as his eulogy. He had written it as if Uncle Nasseem talking about himself and what he was experiencing comparing himself to a leaf that fell from the tree prematurely and was waiting to dry out.

He started to worry that the poem might sound that it's about him and takes away attention from the main reason of being in the funeral which is remembering the one they lost. Few years before, Amir was attending a wedding and the groom's father, stood up to say something about the groom. When the groom's father started reading from the paper in his hand, Amir was not happy with what he heard. The way he wrote his speech was that he wanted to say that the best accomplishment in his life was to see his kids grow up. This could have been a great line if it was written this way. The way the groom's father wrote it was that he listed to the audience his accomplishments in his life which was a whole list of high positions, degrees and awards and then he ended it about his kids. Although it might not have been the groom's father intention to impress the audience with his accomplishments, the way Amir heard it was a list of all what he did in his life and that was it. After that speech, Amir felt that if he ever had to say something in a public event that was about someone else, he had to be careful not to make it sound that it was about him when it should not be. Nevertheless, he decided to work on finishing the poem and ended up saying it in the Funeral.

Tom texted Amir on Friday to let him know that he was coming to the funeral. To Amir's surprise on Saturday morning, Tom came and Debbie came with him. Amir told her that she did not have to come given her health problems, but she said she needed to. Amir had prepared what he was going to say and when the time came in between the prayers Father George asked Amir to come and give his talk. Amir took the paper out of his pocket and stood in front of the Microphone and started:

"Thank you all for coming to share with us saying goodbye to my Uncle Nasseem. As a child growing up in Egypt, I had fun memories with Uncle Nasseem. He came to America 40 something years ago and 15 years later, I came. After he lived with his late brother Dr. Ibrahim, he lived by himself in LI, NY for many years. About three years ago, he started to have memory problems and when he got lost and people found him, he could only remember his brother's widow's name, Debbie, and her phone number and he would tell a stranger to call her. After several events like this, we decided that it was not safe for him to be by himself and he came to NJ to live in a nursing home. He had Alzheimer's or dementia and his memory deteriorated. In his memory, I wrote few lines, imagining him describing how the last few years felt to him considering himself a green leaf that fell off the tree and was waiting to dry out. Please forgive my Egyptian accent and my poor language skills as you listen to what I named, the fallen leaf…"

"The Fallen Leaf.

It's not winter yet, it's not even fall,

I'm losing my connections, I lost my control

I used to be green, with energy and sounds

My energy is fading, I almost touched the grounds

Please don't touch me, just leave me alone

And come closer and help me and please take me home

It's happening so fast and I don't have a clue

My thoughts are disappearing; I can't find my shoe

I am driving and able, I'll find a place to eat

Or maybe I should stop and try another street,

My words are not forming, to silence I am defeat

My pages are blank, but my story isn't complete

Please stop asking me questions, don't know who you are,

I don't know the answers; they left me and went far

If you ever find me, please call a lady, I have her number

Her name is Debbie, she knows me, she'll remember

There is also my nephew, whose name nobody gets

He brought me here and left me, I think he forgets

How long will it take them to watch me dry out?

O Lord please take me, in You, I have no doubt.

I knew, one day I'll go, just like my siblings

Nobody should worry, I have no belongings."

That moment when he finished his speech Amir felt that it was one of his most successful moments in his entire life. He had never recited his own writings in front of a group of people. Having seen many of the Disney movies with his children, it felt to him like the moment when a superhero breaks his fear of showing his powers in front of the people and *"let it go."* The members of the church had prepared a meal for them after they came back from the burial. Amir sat down at one of the tables in the church's social hall next to Debbie, Tom and the two priests who came for the service. Debbie started some conversation with Father George about the Catholic Church and how she was excited about a potential change allowing the priests to marry.

Father George smiled proudly and told her that the Coptic Church had been practicing this from the time the church started. Then Debbie turned to Amir and said, "I liked the burial that you arranged for Nasseem and I told Tom that I wanted something like this." She went on and said, "Remember that you told me that you were not there when your father died and that's one of the reasons you wanted to help Nasseem."

Amir said, "That's true, but I didn't really do much for him." He didn't tell her that he also remembered that she always said that Nasseem should outlive everyone because he always took care of himself and he went to more than one doctor for every organ. How little do we, humans, know about the future when it comes to our day of departure! The Nasseem that she always knew was so much different in the last three years.

The question that remained on Amir's mind all the times was whether he was doing enough for Nasseem. He was very sure that he could have done something better to help him, but how, he didn't know. When his son decided that it was better for him to keep the green fallen leaf in his room, he knew it was going to dry out and die but this, to him, was a little better than having been left on the side walk. Amir's *Fallen Leaf* was not left on the side-walk and was at least protected from some dangers but it had already lost all the connection with what could have kept it alive. Amir tried to convince himself that it had fallen to the ground long before he got it and protected it, until it dried out in peace.

www.ingramcontent.com/pod-product-compliance
Lightning Source LLC
Chambersburg PA
CBHW061516050726
47593CB00002B/601